To my number one J Kathryn

THE KIDS WHO LIVED IN A HOLE

best read with a wee dram

C.G. LAMBERT

This is a work of fiction. Names, characters, places, and incidents either are the product of the author's imagination or are used fictitiously. Any resemblance to actual persons, living or dead, events, or locales is entirely coincidental.

Copyright © 2021 by C.G. Lambert

All rights reserved. No part of this book may be reproduced or used in any manner without written permission of the copyright The Moral Right of the author is asserted.

First paperback edition June 2021

Published by Clamp Ltd

Set in Junicode and Trade Gothic

Cover Art by Nick Castle

Map by Karin Wittig

ISBN 978-1-914531-00-2 Paperback (KDP)

ISBN 978-1-914531-01-9 Hardback

ISBN 978-1-914531-02-6 Paperback (IngramSpark)

ISBN 978-1-914531-03-3 ePUB

www.cglambert.com

www.clamp.pub

For Ange

CONTENTS

Prologue	1
Arrival	3
London	21
The Estate	38
The Duck's Bark	58
Hangover	69
Dinner	76
Ingenue	86
Fire in the Night	97
The Hole	102
The Hole: Part Two	117
Waiting	126
The Plan	140
Executing the Plan	149
Reunion	161
Epilogue	167

ACKNOWLEDGMENTS

Even self-published novels have many people helping—and while every mistake is my own, the following people have been most helpful with their contributions:

Thanks to my beta readers—Andrew Grenfell, Todd Gault, Leah Carson & Ann Donato for their insights and feedback.

Thanks to my Editor, Michael Thorn for his gentle guidance and local knowledge. There are indeed no stone walls in Sussex!

Thanks to Nick Castle for the great cover art and to Karin Wittig for the brilliant map. It's always great when you're dealing with professionals who get what you're trying to do and make it work for you.

And always, thanks to my First Reader.

MAP OF THE EASTWELL ESTATE

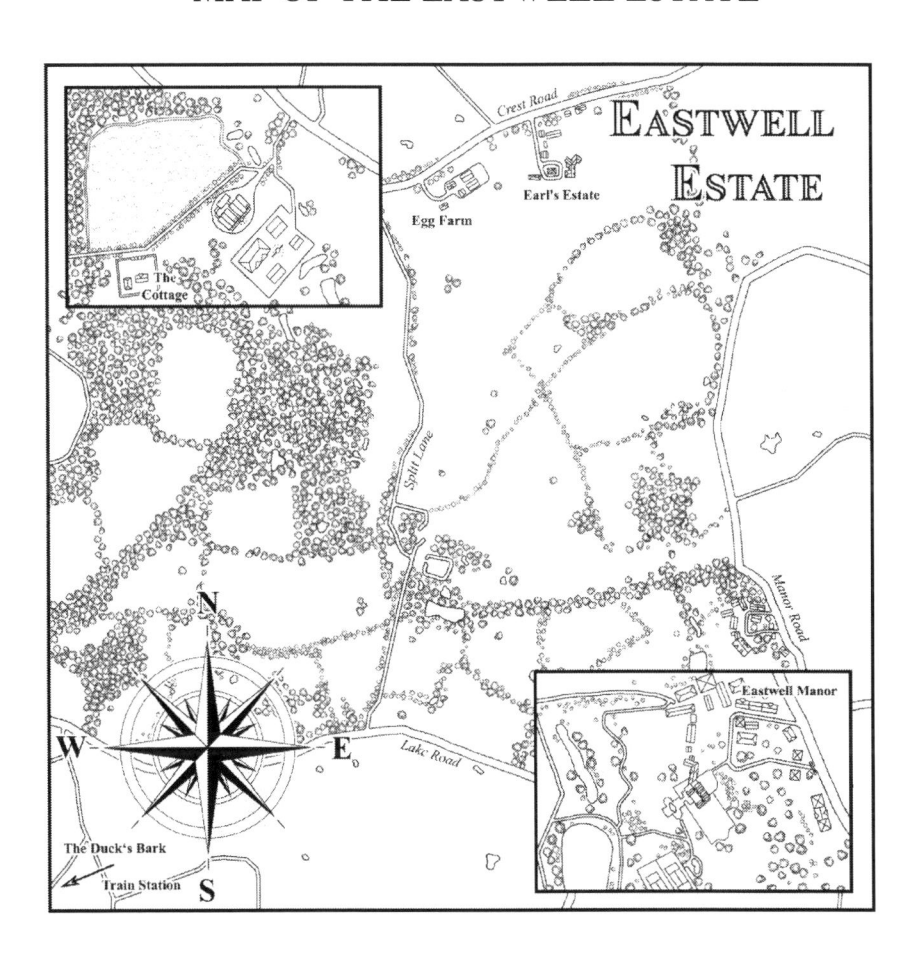

PROLOGUE

The gunshot pierced the night sky. A silhouette in the car headlights twitched and fell. Another shot rang out and the second figure outlined by the lights fell too. Marcus was watching from a great way off but could see perfectly clearly four or five figures in front of the Earl's mansion stop and look towards their position. The threatening clouds that had been accumulating since late afternoon briefly cleared above, allowing a moonbeam to pick them out on the hill opposite the mansion. It was like a stage spotlight showing exactly where Marcus, Zoe and Uncle Reggie were standing, watching from half a mile away. The darkened figures immediately jumped into their cars and started the engines.

"Time to go," urged Uncle Reggie, collecting a hand in each of his and starting down the road back towards their mansion. They broke into a run, Marcus's uncle able to move quite quickly when he got going. Behind them, they could hear tyres screech as their pursuers took corners at breakneck speed. Marcus found himself hoping they would crash.

He chanced a glance behind and saw that the Earl's mansion was ablaze, with half a dozen other properties also aflame. The cars' headlights could be seen driving along Crest Road. Soon they would be turning into Split Lane—the country lane the three of them were running down— and then they would likely meet the same fate as the Earl and his wife.

Uncle Reggie stopped. They had reached the point in Split Lane where they needed to turn off to make their way back to the mansion. But Uncle Reggie had other ideas.

"Marcus, wait. Listen. There's a bunker in the pasture in front of our cottage. You know where the cottage is, right? Take Zoe there until it's safe to come out. The door is hidden, but line up the lights from the fish farm and the power lines and where those lights are on top of each other you'll find a door in the ground. There's enough food in there for a hundred people for a hundred days. The code is Aunt Meredith's birthday. Go quickly! Look after your sister!"

ARRIVAL

Marcus stared out of the window of the old Land Rover, a thousand-yard stare on his fifteen-year-old face. It seemed a lot longer than a 30-minute car ride after twenty-five hours in the air and lacklustre sleep. Idyllic pastures and woodlands flashed by unseen, a bleary streak of green. Aunty Meredith was sitting in the middle of the back seat between him and his younger sister Zoe, who was likewise there but not there, staring trancelike out of her window. They'd felt quite special, walking out at Arrivals to be greeted by Uncle Reggie and Aunty Meredith, with William the groundsman holding up a sign bearing their names. Uncle Reggie and Aunty Meredith looked every bit the odd couple: Uncle Reggie tall as ever, only slightly stooped by age, just a few wisps of hair on an otherwise perfectly bald head and a deep-pile Victorian gentleman's moustache on his top lip. Aunty Meredith was still a petite beauty, a shower of auburn hair cascading below her shoulders with only the odd strand of silver visible. William, probably of similar age, was more thickset. His muscular frame resulting from a lifetime of manual labour was just beginning to turn to flab.

Local time had just turned 10 am as they loaded their bags into the old dark green Land Rover and headed out of the airport short-stay multi-storey. They left the airport surrounds and joined the M25 to bypass London proper and head into the heart of Sussex.

Marcus was tall for a 15-year-old and a bit on the slim side. A dollop of Afro-like hair sat incongruously on his pale face. He wore thick-rimmed glasses and was prone to breakouts of acne. Zoe was slim too, with long straight mousy hair and a smattering of freckles. She was ten but acted a lot younger. She had proved more than a handful on the three flights over from their home in Auckland, New Zealand. Marcus had not been able to sleep much at all while Zoe, when she wasn't being annoying, had taken advantage of her smaller size to curl up on the seat, propped against the window and snored. Marcus was convinced she'd brought every piece of clothing she owned and his persistent memory of the long-haul journey had been trying to keep an eye on her while dragging both their suitcases through the airports. He was hopeful he wouldn't have to look after her much on their holiday.

The stretches of motorway were punctuated periodically by blink-and-you'll-miss-them sliproads with signs for country towns with names so weird that they threatened to take Marcus out of his zen-like state. Picklestone. South Blargsberry. Nether Wallop. And, once they were off the motorway, small parish churches flashed by, they passed through railway overbridges and splashed through wet lanes bordered by tall mature trees meeting high above, making tunnels through both time and space. The most interesting things he saw were the camping store at Gloomsley Heath—looking at first glance like a circus set up in someone's front yard—and the Tudor houses in Lungfield. After that, the lanes became narrower and the trees lining the road thickened and deepened, the ground disappearing under a carpet of moss and leaves. A little way further led to where the banks were built up on either side of the lane, the trees starting to tower above them and the road narrowed to a single lane.

"Are we nearly there?" whined Zoe.

"We're actually already here, Zoe. The land on each side of the road is part of the estate," answered Aunty Meredith. They pulled into a driveway on the right, easing past a number of white cottages set behind hedges. Marcus had imagined that they'd pull into a long driveway and circle an expansive lawn up to a stately mansion so he was a bit surprised that they were effectively driving down a country suburb, lined with hedges instead of fences.

Zoe frowned. "Which one is yours? I thought you had a big house?"

Uncle Reggie was about to answer when they came to an equestrian facility and Zoe squealed. "Horses!!" Her face pressed up to the window and quickly turned to keep the barn in her view as they headed past and on to the house. Once the stables had disappeared from view, she turned back to face the front just as they drove up to the house itself. It was three stories tall with white walls like the Tudor buildings in Gloomsley Heath. Where the Tudor houses at the Heath had shown signs of age and wear, their dark wooden beams bent and bowed, Eastwell Manor was all straight lines. The roof had four impressive chimneys and trees and bushes clustered around the walls, concealing some of them and making the house seem almost part of its natural surroundings. Uncle Reggie smiled and turned in the passenger seat. "Big enough for you?"

William parked in front of a double garage. He grabbed the luggage while the others headed inside. They were greeted in the reception hall by a bustling matron of a similar age to Groundsman William, carrying a tray of cookies fresh from the oven, oven mitts protecting her hands and flour still on her apron. "I'm Francine the Housekeeper. Go ahead and help yourselves to a cookie!"

The warmth and scent of the cookies filled the air as Zoe rammed most of one into her mouth and immediately helped herself to another. "For later," she grinned. Marcus was more polite, taking only one, but he did not need telling twice when Francine suggested he also take another. The gooey chocolate chips' goodness eased the travel-weariness. While he was eating his first cookie, Marcus glanced around. The interiors were white plaster between dark wood beams, the floors black and white tiles, and a wooden staircase headed upstairs covered in a muted apricot runner.

"Come on through to the library and we'll give you the lie of the land," suggested Uncle Reggie. He led them into a large room with fitted bookshelves and a fireplace. A lemon-yellow couch with two pouffes faced the fireplace and a couple of desks sat under the windows at the far end of the room. As in the hall, the room was bathed in natural light—not the dark brooding interior gloom that Marcus had seen on TV period programmes set in Tudor buildings. As Marcus and Zoe made themselves comfortable on the couch, Uncle Reggie unravelled a map on the coffee table.

"So, we've got a bit over 500 acres, laid out very, very roughly like a figure eight knocked on its side. The right-hand loop has the manor house, the horses and cottages, the formal gardens and lakes with woodlands and a bit of forest on the other side of the road. We usually have the house as a B&B—thirteen rooms and the two masters have ensuites, but the local plastic surgery has block booked the whole place for one of their patients for two months. Our agreement with them says we can't accept public bookings, but family can stay and that's why you guys are able to come over. We'll put you two in adjoining rooms away from the patient—she expects her privacy after all!"

"But Uncle Reggie, don't you and Aunt Meredith live in the big house?"

"Uncle Reggie thinks that the money we make from the larger rooms is worth the slight inconvenience of living on the other side of the estate." Aunty Meredith didn't seem to be bitter about this at all, although she did have a wry grin when she mentioned it.

"Ahem, as I was saying... So, the left-hand side is more wooded, it's still got a few fields separated by hedgerows but the majority of it is unspoiled wilderness. A few lakes, that sort of thing. The points of interest on that side are our cottage and meadow." Here he pointed to the extreme left-hand side of the map, almost as far as you could get from the main house. "The power station and the chicken farm. I've also added a fishery here, and an apiary as well."

Zoe wrinkled her nose. "What's an apiary?"

Uncle Reggie smiled, obviously pleased with himself. "Bees. So we've got pastures running cows and sheep. We've got a full-on chicken run, plus the fishery and bees. And horses in the Equestrian Centre."

Craning his neck, Marcus pointed at a collection of buildings not far from the chicken farm. "What's that?"

Uncle Reggie smirked. "That's the neighbours—the Earl of Dormansland. When we moved in, I walked over there to borrow a cup of sugar. It was hilarious the look on their cook's face as I walked over the fields back home, climbing the fences with this cup of sugar."

Aunty Meredith shook her head. "I don't think anyone else thought it was quite as funny as you did," she suggested.

"Apparently he wasn't impressed when we put a chicken farm so close to his estate. He was lucky it wasn't pigs! We've been invited to his estate for dinner this week, so you'll be able to see how the posh people live. Anyways, we've got some other neighbours here," Uncle Reggie continued, pointing to just above the central point of the figure eight. "And some others a bit further away in every direction. If you get bored you can walk up past our cottage here to the North and do laser tag or paintball, and if you're after a little bit of excitement you can do fishing in the lake down here on the southeastern corner or showjumping on one of the horses."

Now he had Zoe's attention.

"Do you have your own horses?"

Uncle Reggie looked slightly embarrassed. "Well, no," he admitted. "But I can have a word with the lady who leases the Centre from us and see if she'll let you ride a bit."

"Oh, yes please! Marcus, I'm going riding, yay!!"

Marcus looked pleased for his sister.

"Plus there are the facilities at the house: we've got two pools, a gym, tennis courts and a couple of kayaks for the lake. I'm trying to get a couple of small sailboats for the lake but I really don't think it's big enough for them. You'd pretty much be tacking the whole time. But if you go to the lake or for a swim, do not drown. That's not a conversation I want to have with your mother!"

He paused to let them take it all in, before continuing. "And we can head into London to see the sights, or go to the beach at Brighton. Or visit one of the stately homes or castles nearby."

"Wow, Uncle Reggie, how much did all this cost?" Zoe asked.

"Well, I got it for a bit of a bargain - I don't think the previous owners knew what they had. Or maybe they were in a spot of bother and needed to cash out, I'm not sure."

"How did you make all your money?"

Marcus started to tell Zoe not to be rude, but Uncle Reggie held up his hand, smiling that it was ok. "What did your Mum say?"

"She said that one of your crazy ideas must have eventually worked, but she didn't know exactly which one."

Uncle Reggie nodded. "I have tried a few things," he allowed. "Can you two keep a secret?" he asked, a little quieter, leaning forward over the map. They nodded, leaning in to hear. "I started trying to be a writer, but I was terrible." Aunty Meredith snorted in agreement. "Terrible, terrible. And then I discovered there was some software which would tell you how good your writing was and how likely it was to sell. Not much use when you're terrible, right? But they had three tiers of use—one that allowed you a single test, one that allowed one test a month for a year, and one that had no restrictions at all. So, I wrote a little bit of computer code that would randomly create one hundred thousand words, because that's what a novel is, right? Create a book of one hundred thousand words, and then automatically send it to the software. I would get the answers back from their software which says how good or bad the book was, and I set up my code to use that feedback to train my code how to write well. I started off with about three months of reports that had various grades in the range F to D, but then the code got better. A lot better. Soon I was generating books with B's and C's. I started to make the code more flexible so I could make it less random and more driven by inputs—make a book that was more romantic, or had more action, less conversation, that sort of thing. After I did that, I got it to focus on certain genres, relearning the difference in rules for the different types of stories and soon I started getting A's. I generated about a hundred grade A stories in ten genres and then the software stopped working. I reached out to the people running the service. I'll buy this from you, I told them. But nothing. I searched and researched for the people responsible but they had literally vanished into thin air. So, I made up ten fake author names, grabbed some pictures from the internet for profile pictures and made up some bogus back story for each book then started sending them out to agents and publishers and eventually they sold. Every year I send out another ten books and every year I get ten checks, and occasionally I'll see one or other on the bestseller list. One reviewer once pointed out that the author they were reviewing looked a little like a young Salvador Dali, because I had literally used an old photo of a young Salvador Dali, but I just replied 'C'est Romanticism, c'est moi!'."

Zoe and Marcus looked blank, so he continued. "I tell you what, it's a lot easier to ignore bad reviews when it's a computer doing the writing!"

Marcus looked astonished. "But didn't you learn anything about writing from all this?" he asked. "Don't you want to write under your own name?"

Now Uncle Reggie looked surprised. "Write myself? Do you know how hard it is to write a book? A hundred thousand words is hard." He glimpsed Aunty Meredith rolling her eyes and collected himself. "Anyways, let's make a plan for the month. We don't have to plan out what you want to do every day, but let's lock in the days that you want to go into London so that you don't reach the end of your holiday and have a whole bunch of things that you wanted to do and never quite got around to doing. Oh! While I remember..." He pulled out two phones, one black and one a light grey, but otherwise identical. "Here's a phone each. They're cheap and nasty but the charge lasts for a month so even if you forget to charge them, they should be fine. I've put in a sim card and the bill is paid for the month that you're here. I've put our numbers in the address book, so you've got mine, Meredith's, the house number and William and Francine's numbers in there. They're not smartphones so nobody can track you or anything, but they are almost indestructible and are small enough to take everywhere. Some parts of the estate are a bit patchy when it comes to coverage, but when we go to London or Brighton, we should be able to keep in contact even if we get separated."

Marcus finished his second cookie and wiped his hands on his shirt before picking up the black phone and turning it over in his hand. It certainly wasn't an iPhone. Way smaller and lighter with awkward curves and a design that a child probably came up with. If any of his fellow students at school back home had come into class with this they would have been mercilessly bullied.

"Thanks," he managed.

"Can I have the black one?" asked Zoe. Marcus swapped with her with a shrug.

"So, in terms of jet lag, it's a good idea if you try and stay awake as long as possible. Make it to dinner time tonight at 7 pm, then you can eat and afterwards go up to your rooms and sleep and you will almost have reset your body clock. If you sleep between now and then there's a good chance you'll be zonked and have a week of naps and sleeping during the day. So, if you can, keep awake. I'll show you where the kitchen is so you can help yourself to food and the cookies, and we can use one of the pools if you like. I like a swim in the morning. Sets you up for the day. Let's show you to your rooms."

Uncle Reggie led the way back out to the Grand Hall. One of the many doors leading off it turned out to reveal a narrower hallway. Towards the end of this hallway one of the doors had been taken off its hinges, leaving a portal to the most amazing aromas Marcus had ever experienced. They trooped in and Marcus and Zoe looked around open-mouthed. It was a kitchen and dining room, with a pair of French doors opening out onto a perfectly manicured lawn. The muted olive-green Aga oven dominated the kitchen section of the room, multiple rings and doors making it look to Marcus like a mutant merging of three or four normal-sized ovens. Hanging above the oven was a selection of brass cooking implements and beside them an array of pots and pans of varying hues ranging from soot black to a gleaming bronze. Shelves of plates crammed the wall space between the stove and the sink, and the space between the fridge and stove was taken with shelves of spices, jars and a variety of plastic containers. Bustling behind the kitchen bench that separated the two parts of the room was Francine, levering a loaf tin out of one side of the oven to plonk it onto the bench. The delicious smell of freshly baked bread was added to the chaotic pre-existing background smells.

"Francine, I was just telling the kids that they can help themselves to anything in the kitchen. They're fighting jet lag so I figured eating might be one way of keeping them awake. Is anything off-limits?"

"Well, we've only the one paying mouth to feed, so there's plenty to go around. If they help themselves to the fridge in the kitchen, that should be fine," she said, indicating the fridge in the corner of the room.

"You've got more than one fridge?" asked Zoe.

Francine smiled broadly, and beckoned them to follow her. Back across the narrow hall they trooped. Through the door facing the gap to the kitchen they went into another kitchen with even more cupboards and bench space. A pair of double fridges sat against one wall, but Francine was already leading them out of the room and through a door beyond into what turned out to be the laundry. A door in the laundry revealed a larder stacked with shelves holding all sorts of bags, boxes and drums.

"I'm not sure when the apocalypse is coming, but we're well-stocked to wait it out," she said with her ready grin. "One fridge in the kitchen, two large ones in the Butler's Pantry and all this in the larder. With what we grow in the vegetable garden and greenhouses here, the eggs from the farm and the fish from the fishery, our food costs are surprisingly low. Oh, and every now and again William will bag a rabbit."

"Oh no, not a bunny!" squealed Zoe.

"Yeah, sometimes William will bag one and then as sure as eggs are eggs, we'll get a group of vegetarians through who won't touch it," said Uncle Reggie. "We eat well those nights! So, anything in the kitchen is fair game, but anything in the pantry or larder you'll have to check with Francine."

They headed back to the narrow hall and beside the Butler's Pantry was a doorway that led to a different set of stairs. Less grand than the staircase in the Reception Hall, they nevertheless shared the same dark wood and apricot runner. These stairs needed electric lights as there was very limited windowlight. Lamps on L-shaped brackets were attached to the walls with lampshades to soften the light. They headed up the stairs, pausing on the landing on the first floor. Aunty Meredith pointed up the stairs where they continued upwards.

"Six more bedrooms and three bathrooms up there, but your bedrooms are through here."

They opened the door to the first floor and turned right. Three doors led off the corridor in front of them. Behind them, more doors lined the landing. The doors in front of them turned out to have numbers —a 6 and a 7, with the letter B on the third door. They opened room 6 first.

It was huge—easily half again as big as Marcus' room back home. It was almost square, with a large window looking out of over the lawns. Everything in the room was blue—the walls, the curtains, the couch covering and bedspread. All different shades and patterns. Definitely a boy's room, Marcus decided. Apart from the bed and couch there was a wooden dresser and a desk at the window with a giant round mirror on it. A few generic pictures hung in ornate frames on the walls. Marcus walked over to the desk and looked down to the lawns below. From this vantage point he could see that the space in front of the house wasn't featureless. There was a formal garden laid out immediately in front of the house with a circular fountain in the centre. A wide paved path led down to the fountain and then beyond. It stopped at the edge of the lawns and through the trees beyond he could just make out a lake. In the distance, there was pasture and on the horizon, trees. He realised from the map they'd seen in the library that as far as the eye could see was part of the estate.

"Is this one bigger than number 7?" asked Zoe.

"I think that it is" answered Aunty Meredith, frowning slightly.

"Bags this one then!" claimed Zoe.

Marcus shrugged and went to see where he'd be staying. Opening the door to number 7, the first thing he noticed was that William had left both of their suitcases there. The second thing he noticed was that this room was both longer and narrower than number 6, so it was hard to see if it was that much smaller. Maybe only just, he decided. The decor was exactly like that in number 6, and he suspected that the pictures on the wall were exactly the same too. He wondered if his uncle had bought a job lot from some factory that churned out knock off prints of watercolour classics. He looked out of the window. It was a little smaller than Zoe's but fundamentally provided the same view. He turned to his right. Surely, being the end room, there should have been windows on two sides of the room? Apparently not. His room at least did have a built-in closet, rather than a dresser. He took Zoe's bag out and into her room where she was finishing regaling Uncle Reggie and Aunt Meredith with one of her rambling stories that tended to just sort of peter out.

"Here's your bag," he announced to the room, placing it on the ground near the bed. Smiling in gratitude for Marcus having interrupted Zoe's story, Uncle Reggie moved towards the door.

"Grab your togs and I'll show you where the pools are," he said. "We'll wait for you back in the kitchen. If you wanted to freshen up, the bathroom is…"

"The one with the B on the door," finished Marcus, smiling.

Uncle Reggie nodded and he and Aunt Meredith headed back downstairs.

"Do you need toilet?" he asked Zoe.

"I'm not a baby," she frowned, miffed at his choice of words. In all honesty he did baby her, a habit formed by having to look after her a lot and her being five years his junior but looking and acting a lot younger than her ten years.

"Fine. Do you need to use the toilet?" he elaborated.

She paused. "Yeah, I do. I'll meet you downstairs," she said, already heading towards the bathroom door.

"OK, but don't forget your togs," he reminded her, already heading back to his room to get his own swimming costume from his suitcase. He didn't know how long she'd be, so thought he'd go the long way back downstairs and check out the rest of the floor to get his bearings. After digging out his togs, he paused at his door. Should he lock it? The key was in the lock, a thick wooden tag swinging from the loop and a giant 7 burned into the dark stained wood on both sides. What's the chance of the plastic surgery patient being a thief, he thought. Unlikely, unless she was a thief getting plastic surgery to change her appearance because she was on the run. And even then, what would she be able to get from the clothing and toiletries of a fifteen-year-old boy, er, man, from the other side of the world? Realising he was letting the jet lag get to him, Marcus decided to err on the side of caution and locked the door, putting the key in his jeans pocket and started walking down the corridor.

Going past the door to the stairs, he dawdled, soaking up time. Another B on the left, then 5 on the right directly opposite another B on the left. One last B on the left before the left-hand side of the hallway disappeared into the void overlooking the main staircase. Opposite the staircase were 4 and then 3 and the corridor ended just after the stairway landing with 1 and 2. The large windows in the reception hall did a good job illuminating the hallway at this end of the house, showing the same generic watercolour paintings and the occasional oval mirror on the walls.

He headed down the master stairs, noting how they didn't go up any further, only servicing the ground and first floor. He guessed that the staircase closer to his room was the only one that did go up to the top floor and, even though these stairs were much better lit and wider than his, he actually preferred his ones as they went straight from his room to the kitchen. Reaching the bottom, he poked his head into the other rooms which opened off the reception hall. Each had an open door, so he figured it was alright.

Three doors led off to the south, two to the east and the hallway to the kitchen to the west. The main entrance door was behind him to the north. The middle of the three southward-facing doors led into the Library where Uncle Reggie had shown them the map, so Marcus poked his head into the doorway between the library and the hallway to the kitchen.

It was a formal dining room, featuring a long table set for six. On one of the lengthwise walls was a huge oil landscape surrounded by a thick golden frame, and opposite that was a fireplace recessed into the wall. At the far end was a window facing the gardens, the curtains pulled back, allowing substantial light to flood the room. A substantial chandelier hung from one of the dark cross beams in the ceiling.

On the other side of the library from the dining room was the Garden Room. Marcus noticed that just above the door jamb was a wooden plaque with the name of the room. "Handy," he muttered as he looked into the Garden Room. This was also a long and narrow room, but whereas the dining room had only a small window overlooking the lawns and fountain, the Garden Room had floor to ceiling windows which really did allow a great view of the gardens. The furniture here was almost beachy, with wicker chairs around a coffee table and even a pair of sun loungers. A myriad of plants made the glass windows seem like a temporary and flimsy barrier between the inside and outside.

Carrying on his counter-clockwise route, Marcus entered the Drawing Room. He figured this must have been renovated at some point in the not too distant past as the ceilings did not feature the dark wood beams and white ceiling boards of the rest of the house, instead being painted plain white. They did have fancy swirling parts at the edges of the ceiling where it joined the walls. The room was filled with numerous comfortable looking couches, each with a reading lamp nearby, angled to shine on whatever was being read on the couch. A grand piano was at the far end of the room, and a grandfather clock stood against one of the walls next to the eastward facing window. Illuminating the room were two sets of windows, the ones on the right looked south, clearly showing the fountain and garden in that direction. The other looked out to the east and he could make out a pool house and a kidney-shaped pool, beyond which was a tennis court. The room was completed by a fireplace on the north wall.

The final room beckoned, and Marcus completed the circuit by entering the Sitting Room. This room was bathed in darkness as the curtains were pulled across the windows on both the north and east sides. It looked like a fireplace was on the south wall, but there was no flame. A couch in the middle of the room faced it and although the room was too dark to really detect colours, Marcus got the impression that the walls of the room and the couch were both the same shade of custard yellow.

"Oh, hello," came a female voice.

Marcus started, realising someone was sitting in the dark. She was slim, wearing a dressing gown and heavily bandaged around the head. She had a ukulele in her hands and was sitting in an armchair in the corner. Marcus had no idea how tall she was, but her voice was rich and vibrant.

"Oh! Sorry to interrupt! I was just looking around," he managed, and quickly made his way back to the kitchen. By the time he got there Zoe had made her way back down with togs in hand and Uncle Reggie and Aunt Meredith led them to the far end of the narrow hallway and outside. Marcus didn't think to mention meeting the bandaged patient in the Sitting Room.

The path outside separated the raised vegetable beds on the left from the glasshouses on the right, and the walls of the glasshouses weren't too high to prevent Marcus and Zoe looking inside at an impressive arrangement of trees and shrubbery.

"What's Francine growing at the moment?" asked Uncle Reggie, pausing to peer through the glass.

Aunty Meredith was a little shorter so stood on tippy toes. "I think she mentioned that she can get avocados to grow in there and there's also some mangos and pineapple. I don't think the bananas are growing too well, but there's always some oranges and mandarins. I think they call those clementines here."

Marcus looked at the assorted lush greenery in the raised beds on the opposite side of the path and wondered if anyone could distinguish between the different types of greenery from just what was growing above ground. He certainly couldn't.

Just beyond the glasshouses they came across the entrance to the swimming pool and Uncle Reggie pointed out where they could get changed and where the gym was. The pool itself was enormous, with a vaulted ceiling and a pair of pipes running the length of the ceiling. Against the wall on the side opposite the entrance was a garden of sorts, several cactus plants and spiky-leaved ferns growing in pots in a row, some of them reaching up above the level of the ceiling and making the austere interior a little more friendly.

"Through there is the entrance to the Equestrian Centre," pointed Uncle Reggie, Zoe swinging around with laser-like focus. "I'll have a chat with her this afternoon and see if she'll let you ride. She might want you to help out with the horses though, in exchange. Would that be ok?"

Marcus thought Zoe might have a stroke. She managed a nod, grinning maniacally.

"OK, so that's the indoor pool, but we've also got an outdoor pool. Come this way!" He led the way back past the gardens towards the house. Instead of taking them back inside, he took them through the formal garden with the fountain and around past the whole southern-facing part of the house to the pool house and the kidney-shaped pool that Marcus had seen from his explorations. Aunty Meredith ducked back into the house as they passed the door to the kitchen and rejoined them soon after with a pair of laptops under her arm.

Uncle Reggie pointed out the pool house. "So, you can get changed in there and there are also some tennis racquets and tennis balls for the tennis courts if you want to have a knock around. I warn you; I will not take mercy on you if we play tennis! If we get hungry, the phone on the wall has a direct connection to the kitchen, and the water isn't too cold when the sun's out like this. Any time after about October it gets a little too cold for my liking, but I usually use the indoor pool anyway because it's just a little bit longer so you swim further."

"Are you or Aunty Meredith going to swim with us?"

"I'm afraid we both have a bit of work to do but we'll be just here on the loungers. I know that Francine will need a hand with dinner and…"

"And the hor…" started Zoe

"And I need to find out about the horses," agreed Uncle Reggie. "So plenty to do!"

They'd managed to fight through jet lag by staying up all day, playing in the pool first before getting dressed and trying out the tennis court. They'd taken Uncle Reggie's warning to heart and decided to just play tennis between themselves instead of involving the adults. There was a significant difference in skill between Marcus and Zoe which had led to a brief but spirited change in game from a variant of tennis to a variant of dodgeball. Afterwards they'd been quite worn out and had made their way back up to the house for some lunch.

They didn't have to raid the fridge after all, as Francine was waiting with plates of ploughman's lunches—the fresh bread they'd seen her taking out of the oven, topped with slices of cheese, ham and a slathering of relish. After lunch, Uncle Reggie and Aunt Meredith had headed back to their cottage to do some work and so Zoe and Marcus watched a movie in the Drawing Room, Francine providing truffle oil popcorn. After the movie Francine had kept them busy helping make dinner and before they knew it Uncle Reggie and Aunt Meredith had returned from their cottage and they all reconvened in the library. Between the four of them they decided that they'd take a day trip into London the next day, giving ample opportunity to revisit in case they missed anything the first time. They listed all of the things that they wanted to see, and Uncle Reggie worked out the route between all of them. The only thing they wouldn't be able to do was check out the changing of the guard at Buckingham Palace, the ceremony occurring well after they planned to pass by that location. Aunt Meredith promised that they'd be able to go back on a different day to see it. She also had some good news about the horse riding, telling Zoe that if she was keen on riding, the lady who ran the Equestrian Centre would be happy to swap rides for help mucking out the stables and general dogsbody work. Marcus didn't say anything but he wondered if that arrangement would fall foul of any child labour laws. Zoe looked happy at the arrangement, and Marcus supposed that if she came back from the first day unhappy, then she wouldn't have to go back. It wasn't like she was going up the chimneys or down the mines. The thought of Zoe covered in soot from either activity struck him as funny and he let out a snort. They all looked at him and to distract them he got to his feet.

"Shall we see Francine about dinner?"

LONDON

The booklet in Marcus's room mentioned that breakfast was available between 8 and 9 each morning, unless otherwise requested. They had an earlier start in mind than that, and had got up at 7 am to have a full cooked English breakfast perched on stools at the counter between the kitchen and the dining area. Marcus had slept like a log as soon as his head had hit the pillow, waking when the sun had peeked through the blinds and then dozing for another hour before the alarm went off. Zoe also reported having had a satisfactory night's sleep. Francine quizzed them on what they were going to see and why, finding out their itinerary and offering her opinions which were long on "that's a beautiful building" and short on any sort of critique. She was quickly becoming a favourite of both Zoe and Marcus.

After washing and brushing their teeth, they re-assembled at the garage and following a last-minute check that they each had their phones, they got into the cavernous Land Rover with William once again navigating the country roads. Marcus noticed that while Francine was all friendly warmth and bustle, William was more taciturn, not offering much in terms of opinion, but pleasant enough. After a five minute trip, he dropped them off at East Felstead train station and, with a tip of his cap, drove off back towards the Manor.

Uncle Reggie bought the tickets at the counter, handing them each their Oyster cards, admonishing them not to lose them and, before he knew it, Marcus was on the train heading into London. Being brought up on Harry Potter, he was a little disappointed that the train was modern and not steam-driven, and that they wouldn't be arriving at one of the more famous stations like Kings Cross or St Pancras. But he could feel excitement rising as they left the pastures and farmland behind and started to pass through the city suburbs with their trackside allotments, then semi-industrial areas, and finally restricted views of high rise apartments. Marcus noticed two other things as they got closer to the city—they'd started on a double line well above ground level with the occasional bridge over the road and by the time they'd reached the city they were looking at embankments on either side of the rail line as if they were descending into the earth. The sheer number of rails beside theirs had also exploded in number.

They emerged from the train in Victoria Station, a cavernous space teeming with other passengers streaming off other trains or running to catch trains about to leave. The chaos was a little overwhelming. Marcus made sure to keep one eye on Zoe to ensure she didn't wander off, while he kept the other on Uncle Reggie. It helped that Uncle Reggie was taller than most of the other people around so served as a good navigational aid. Having an eye on two different people meant he wasn't really watching where he was going and almost walked into an armed policeman.

"Steady on, pal," the policeman warned in a deep Scottish accent, both hands on his automatic weapon and watching with a steely gaze. Behind him was another similarly-armed policeman, also keeping a wary eye on him. As he manoeuvred past them, he noticed that they both had bulletproof vests on. It was a bit of a shock as the policemen back home weren't normally armed and here they had machine guns! He caught up with the others and they got through the ticket barriers and headed towards the exit.

"Our Visitor cards mean we can go on any bus, Underground or ferry in the city all day," Uncle Reggie told them. "We don't know what time we'll start getting tired, so it's good to have a backup plan for getting around. Onwards ho!" He seemed to be enjoying himself. Marcus didn't know whether it was the planning or playing tour leader, but there was a distinct bounce in Reggie's step. He led the way out of the station, through the crowds and onto the streets. A steady stream of black cabs and red buses made their way past the station, some of them disgorging passengers at random locations and times, others picking up people without rhyme or rhythm. Marcus found the chaos marginally easier to manage than inside the station and easier to keep close to Uncle Reggie by tucking into the slipstream that he made as he walked down the street. Zoe followed straight after him and Aunty Meredith brought up the rear. They progressed in formation until the crowds diminished a little and Marcus could look around more. The pavement they followed had some sort of historical buildings on the other side of the street, but this side was non-stop souvenir shops and fast-food takeaways. Then, without warning, the road turned slightly and the demeanour of the neighbourhood changed entirely. From the bustling commercial feel of the area around the station where they'd arrived to the tourist shops of the preceding section, now there was the side of a grand building on the left-hand side of the road and enormous stately homes on the right. The stately homes were all in variations of the same colour scheme, with the pillars and walls painted a slightly off white and the metal railings painted a contrasting black. Both sides of the street were now lined with mature trees and the streets themselves were teeming with tourist buses, big red TFL buses, black cabs and delivery vans. They could now walk near each other and Marcus caught Uncle Reggie's eye.

"What is that place over there?" he asked, indicating the grand building on the left side of the road.

"Ah, that's the side of Buckingham Palace," he answered. "I took your grandmother there when she came over and visited."

Marcus snorted and then saw that Uncle Reggie was serious.

"Yeah, before they locked down the Royal family, they would let the public through the State Rooms and have a look around the Palace. Not while the Queen was in there or anything, and they kept a sharp eye on the groups, but it was a nice little earner for them. Granny loved it! You know she loves the Royal family so she was in her element. Can't do that now of course."

They'd reached an intersection and crossed over the road to the left, leaving the shelter of the trees lining the footpaths to walk on the path. The road was now coloured a rust red and exposed to the sun. There'd been some sort of gate or barrier which prevented vehicle access, so now the street noise was just what their fellow tourists were making. Marcus was surprised at the difference that made. The fencing on their left hiding the Palace was almost twenty feet high and was stout black metal topped with gold. It wasn't much of a walk before they were in the gigantic plaza with a huge fountain in the middle of it which offered the familiar views of Buckingham Palace that Marcus recognised from TV and film. The gates and fences emblazoned with the royal family's crest were maybe thirty feet high. On the other side of the fence, there was a broad expanse of open area before the Palace proper. Guardsmen stood in the shade of little boxes against the wall of the Palace, occasionally stomping a little way from the box, then doing an elaborate turn and then returning, their rifle bayonets glinting in the sunlight.

The four of them formed a little knot near the fence so that the kids could see the Palace in all its glory and they could hear each other. It was a truly huge building and with the open area in front of it they could fully appreciate its size. Marcus noticed more armed police at one end of the building, manning a station a little way removed from the Guardsmen's boxes.

"Uncle Reggie, why do they need the police if they have the army?"

"Good question," responded Uncle Reggie, looking around to see if anyone was listening and crouching down so he could reply quietly. "So I don't know the reason, but the police are the only ones allowed loaded firearms. The Guardsmen you can see there are ceremonial."

"But does that mean if bad men try and do anything that they won't be able to protect the Queen?" Zoe asked.

"Oh, no!" replied Uncle Reggie. "See that shiny bit on the end of their gun? Now that's real. And sharp. So that will do some damage. And whether they're loaded or not, you've got a hundred guys who are chosen for their loyalty and who are constantly training in hand-to-hand combat whose job it is to protect the Queen and they're all between her and the bad guys. So if they manage to get past the armed police, they still have to deal with the army guys. So they don't have to be loaded. It was funny when Granny and I visited. The ending of the tour dumps you into the cafe on the other side of the building and you can sit there and look out at the grounds for as long as you like. When you're finished they take you through to this side on a golf cart and drop you off at that gate over there. When we got dropped off, there was a tourist group who were convinced we must have been semi-royalty leaving after seeing the Queen, so they were taking all sorts of photos of us. Mum gave them all her best Royal wave."

"I wish they still let people inside."

"Maybe one day, Zoe. Have you guys seen enough?"

"What's the statue?" Marcus had turned his back on the Palace and was facing the centre of the plaza.

"That's Victory," answered Uncle Reggie. "This is where Britons come to celebrate the end of wars, weddings, births, that sort of thing."

"I thought it was the Queen Victoria Monument," frowned Aunty Meredith.

"...anyways, have we seen enough, kids?" Uncle Reggie asked, one eye on his watch. After a chorus of "Yes" and "I guess", they headed away from the statue-of-many-names into the nearby park. A large lake lay in the centre of it, periodically obscured from view by the wide variety of trees and bushes, making the walk along the path through the park a delightful change from all the man-made mansions, roads and traffic. There was still a steady stream of tourists heading in both directions, some groups with a guide at the front, holding an umbrella or a sign or in one case a stick with a stuffed unicorn on top. Occasionally the tour guide would have a headset and the group would be a little more dispersed, listening intently on headphones. Marcus expected at any time they would break out into synchronised dance steps, equating the microphone on the headset with the stage microphones used by performers at concerts.

The early morning cloud cover had started to lift and the breeze was soft enough to still be pleasant, so all their jackets were still in Uncle Reggie's backpack.

"What's this park called?" asked Zoe, as they passed a group of tourists feeding swans from the bank, in direct contravention of the sign right beside them explicitly prohibiting the practice.

Uncle Reggie sounded very sure of himself as he answered that it was very definitely St James' Park, and Marcus noticed the corner of Aunt Meredith's mouth twitch into a semi-smile. Before long, they left the park and headed back into the streets, marvelling at the huge mansions looming over the traffic below. Periodically Zoe would read a plaque or date embedded in a building and exclaim how old the building or event was. There were fewer tourists along these roads, but the level of pedestrian traffic hadn't decreased, and most of the flow was heading in the direction that they were headed. Marcus noticed a worried look flash between Uncle Reggie and Aunty Meredith as they too detected a change in the air.

At the end of the street that they were walking along, they saw two large trees, one on each side of the road, their leaves and branches intertwined high above. Their archway seemed to indicate the entrance to somewhere grand and beyond Marcus could make out an expanse of blue sky indicating some sort of square or open park ahead. As they got closer they could hear a low hubbub of crowds talking like you'd get at a fete or a fair and when they reached the trees they had a better idea of what was going on.

A square park was surrounded by the road, and in the middle of it was a growing crowd. Some people were preparing placards with various slogans on them, some were standing around talking and some were listening to a man on a stone step who was giving an impassioned yet indecipherable speech. Marcus couldn't tell at this distance whether he was even speaking English, let alone making sense, and judging from the body language of those around him, the audience was similarly confused. The vibe in the square was relaxed, with maybe an undercurrent of anticipation. The roads had no traffic on them, so they skirted the park proper and made their way around to the other side.

"That's Westminster Abbey," said Aunty Meredith, pointing to the enormous church set back from the footpath and surrounded by a lovely flat lawn. A snake of tourists waiting for entry wended its way along the outside wall, under the watchful gaze of a couple of unarmed police officers. "That's where the Royal family gets married and christened."

They continued on, turning right away from the square and pulled up short. It seemed that they had found the epicentre of the protest. About the same number of people who were on the square behind them, preparing placards, were in front of them at the gates of the ornate palace which Marcus instantly recognised as the Houses of Parliament.

"And that's where Parliament sits," Aunty Meredith said.

"I think that's as close as we should probably go," said Uncle Reggie. In the distance, beyond the mass of protestors, Marcus could make out police vans and mounted police officers. Behind the black wrought iron fences (lower than those around Buckingham Palace) were clusters of pairs of police officers displaying relaxed body language with their firearms slung across their chests, but with wary eyes endlessly moving this way and that under their peaked caps.

"Where's Big Ben?" asked Zoe.

"Good point, it's back this way," said Uncle Reggie and they headed back towards the square before hanging right. Ahead of them was a bridge over the Thames and to the left a weird building that combined Tudor style with a modern metal and glass construction, but their attention was taken by the towering clock tower to their right. They stood to the side of the footpath to let others past and stared.

Beside them, a couple of young men were also discussing the clock tower and Marcus couldn't help but overhear their conversation.

"Did you know that what we're seeing is not actually Big Ben?" started the first.

"It certainly looks like all the photos I've seen," countered the second.

"I mean that Big Ben is actually the bell inside the tower that we're looking at," elaborated the first.

"But when people talk about Big Ben they mean the tower and the bell."

"Well then they're wrong - the bell is Big Ben and the tower which holds it is the Elizabeth Tower."

"Meh, sometimes words change meanings and names change what they refer to. Like Gary used to mean 'my mate' and now it means 'pedantic knob-end'."

Uncle Reggie cleared his throat and asked the children if they were ready to move on, and so they headed towards the bridge. More souvenir kiosks lined the footpaths, Union flags, I love London sweatshirts, hats and scarves hung from makeshift stalls.

"We'll go to Number 10 Downing Street a different day," suggested Uncle Reggie. "I had a look down towards it when we crossed the street and it looked like the street was blocked with protestors, so we'll come back when things are a little less hectic."

"Ooh! A ferris wheel!" exclaimed Zoe, indicating the London Eye on the other side of the river.

"Um, look I don't want to be cheap, but it's not all that it's cracked up to be. You pretty much see the same view of London for an hour, admittedly from a slightly different height. Let's keep going." Uncle Reggie led them down the Embankment along the riverside, partly shaded by tall trees. This side of the river was less crowded than the side with the Eye. They could see that even this early in the morning there were significant crowds. Zoe spotted the ferry stop on their side of the river.

"Oh! Can we go on the boat?" she squealed.

"Maybe later. It does connect a lot of the things on our list, and it is covered by our ticket," admitted Uncle Reggie. That seemed to satisfy Zoe and they continued along, enjoying the openness of being by the River.

As they came opposite the Eye, they noticed the rumbling noise of many people yelling to their left. Uncle Reggie craned his neck and told them that they were hearing the protest outside Number 10. The yelling didn't sound too angry and periodically there was laughter as well, so Marcus figured it was the warm-up act for whatever else the protestors had in mind for the Houses of Parliament.

Onwards they walked, past a ship in the river which had been repurposed as a pub, and turned left parallel to a rail line which had just crossed the river in front of them. They were now back in what Marcus was realising was standard inner-city London. Wide footpaths with trees embedded in them, five or six storey grand buildings built between two and three hundred years ago, and very well kept.

They popped out the end of the road into an enormous open area. Directly in front of them was a roundabout with a statue of a man on a horse in the middle of it, but the larger open area on the right was what held their attention.

"The Lions!" shrieked Zoe and as soon as the lights at the intersection changed she was off across the road and clambering aboard one of the giant lion statues at the base of Nelson's column. The other three wandered over in good time and as they did so Marcus' attention was attracted by yet another large gathering of people, clustered at the other end of the Square under the pillars in the middle of the statuesque building. On the steps, a man with a megaphone was yelling to a group of hundreds of placard carriers. Marcus watched for a while but the message was lost as the noise drifted across the Square, so he turned back towards Zoe. She had apparently become bored on the Lion and was heading back down.

"Can we take the bus? My feet are getting tired!" she complained.

Uncle Reggie consulted his map and suggested that they could take the ferry instead.

"Yay!"

They headed back the way they had come, going under the rail bridge and discovering another ferry stop on a floating pontoon accessed via a ramp heading down from the Embankment. The tide must have been out because the ramp was quite steep, and they had to hold the bannister. They were lucky with the timing and one ferry was just pulling into the station, disgorging its passengers before allowing the next set on. There was only one section for sitting, so they filed in and grabbed a set of four seats together. The ferry was about half full and it didn't take the ticket inspector long to get around to them, touching each of their Oyster Cards to his machine and nodding at the little green light that came up.

From the low tide level, the city loomed over them and the view through the windows was mostly of wooden poles and pilings. Here and there they could see patches of mud at the banks, and someone was actually walking around on one section, the mud coming up to mid-calf.

They headed towards a bunch of bridges but Uncle Reggie warned them that they were only going one stop, which turned out to be on the other side of the river, so they were ready to get off as the ferry approached Bankside. After they got off, Uncle Reggie turned to them and asked if they were hungry. "Time for a picnic, then," he said when they allowed that they might be just a little peckish.

As they walked past an old white round building, Aunt Meredith told them that it was actually a reconstruction of The Globe, a theatre where

Shakespeare had shown his plays back in the day. Uncle Reggie wryly told them that no matter how much anyone begs not to watch the play from ground level "standing up for three hours is bloody tiring", and even if they did get seats to take along a pillow or cushion because "Shakespeare's seats are bloody uncomfortable".

Aunt Meredith elbowed him. "You enjoyed it!"

To which Uncle Reggie begrudgingly agreed.

Ahead of them, a pedestrian footbridge crossed the river, coming ashore between them and an enormous brick building with a towering chimney. Peeking between buildings on the other side of the river, with the pedestrian footbridge pointing directly towards it was a domed building gleaming white against the surrounding greys and browns. As they got closer to the brick building with the tower, Uncle Reggie told them that it was Tate Modern and it used to be a power station and that the domed building on the other side of the bridge was St Paul's Cathedral, where the icons of British society were buried. Neither building had featured on Marcus' or Zoe's lists of places that they wanted to visit so, instead, they used the grass in front of the Tate as the setting for a picnic, opening the Tupperware boxes of sandwiches and snacks that Francine had given them before they had set off that morning.

After they'd settled in and were each on their second sandwich (egg salad), Marcus asked about the protests.

"What were all those protests about?" he said between bites.

Aunt Meredith and Uncle Reggie shared a look. "Well," he started, "from the placards I read, the one at Parliament was generally about poverty, the one at Number 10 was calling on one of the ministers to be sacked for some sort of scandal and the one at Trafalgar Square was about a particular benefits policy."

"What's poverty?" asked Zoe.

"I think it's not having sufficient money to buy enough food to eat, a place to live or clothes to wear," Marcus tried, looking uncertain at Uncle

Reggie.

"I don't want to oversimplify things," responded Uncle Reggie, "but yeah, it's not having enough."

"Not having enough is bad," asserted Zoe, looking serious.

"That's true, and there are huge disagreements on how to define that, who should fix it and the best way to fix it. That's why people get angry and go to protests, because some people think that there's nothing wrong and those that do think there is something wrong disagree on how to fix it. Are you ready to continue? We've still got London Bridge and the Tower to go."

They packed the containers away and got the jackets out. The clouds had thickened and the breeze freshened, dropping the temperature a few degrees. Aunty Meredith dropped her crusts into the nearby rubbish bin and they all took drinks out of a large bottle of water.

"Might as well get our money's worth from the tickets," Uncle Reggie said as they made their way the short distance back to the ferry stop. The bridge across from the Tate to St Paul's was popular, with the end particularly congested with tourists looking for the perfect picture and the ensuing crowding subsequently ensuring that nobody did. They weren't as lucky this time around and had a fifteen-minute wait for the next boat. When it did arrive it was more densely packed and they could only find three seats together. They decided that since they were only going one stop that they should just stand near the entrance, leaning against the wall separating the awning-covered rear from the passenger compartment for support. As a result, they were the first ones off after they pulled into the stop. The water looked positively brown now, and the muddy riverbed very clearly exposed at the edges.

The paths along the riverside were modern and in stark contrast to the historic city they had been moving through up to that point. A warship lay just off the bank, connected by a walkway and, in the distance, the most famous ornate bridge crossing the Thames stood with its arms raised to allow a high-masted sailing ship to pass beneath. Marcus had started in that direction before Uncle Reggie called out after him.

"I thought you wanted to see London Bridge?"

Marcus turned confused. 'Isn't that it?" he asked. "It looks like all the pictures."

"Nope, that's Tower Bridge," answered Uncle Reggie, "London Bridge is that one," pointing to the bridge in the opposite direction.

Marcus looked at the bridge in question. Describing it as non-descript would not be enough. It was as devoid of ornament and style as Tower Bridge was imbued with both. It was almost an anti-Tower Bridge—everything one was, the other was not.

Uncle Reggie smirked. "I thought you might have made that mistake. No big deal. Some Americans also made that mistake and bought 'London Bridge'. Reassembled it back in the US. Would have loved to see their face when they saw it. 'I spent how much on that?'"

They headed towards Tower Bridge along the paths that hugged the riverbank, passing an assortment of restaurants with alfresco seating overlooking the river. They then passed the entrance to the warship which turned out to be a cruiser named HMS Belfast. Then the neighbourhood changed again, switching to an open plaza surrounded by glass and steel office towers. They were close enough now to have a really good view of both Tower Bridge and the glistening white Tower of London on the other side of the river. The arms of the bridge were now lowering, the queues of waiting vehicles waiting patiently.

Uncle Reggie smiled at him, reading his thoughts. "The old and the new, right? The modern offices and Armadillo," he indicated a weirdly shaped glass oval building very nearby, "opposite the Tower, and the modern cars and buses on the Tower Bridge."

They climbed the steps up from riverside level to bridge level and started walking along the bridge itself. They got to about halfway along and Zoe looked up and frowned.

"Are those windows up there?" she asked, pointing to the upper arms connecting the inner towers of the bridge.

The others followed her pointing finger and could make out some of the sections of the connecting arms didn't have the same lattice structure as the other parts and instead had glass with lights beyond. Occasionally the view of the light would flicker as if someone was walking between it and the window.

"You can go on a tour and walk across those passageways and part of it has a glass floor, allowing you to see the traffic and pedestrians below," admitted Aunty Meredith. "We can come back for that if you like. I think you have to book your tickets."

Marcus wasn't sure he'd like that but Zoe seemed keen. They continued on to their final stop, the Tower of London, leaving the bridge via stairs which popped them out in a tunnel underneath. From there it was a stroll along a cobbled path to the entrance of the castle, with a little wait while Uncle Reggie went on ahead to get the tickets from the ticket booths which were awkwardly placed further away.

When he returned, they headed inside and spent a good few hours wandering around the various exhibits. They smirked at the armour of King Henry VIII, the codpiece excessively prominent and unrealistically large. They clambered through the narrow openings in the Bloody Tower and they marvelled at the Royal Mint. Eventually, they went through the Jewel House and queued behind a family of Indian extraction. They stood on the moving conveyor belt as it rotated past the jewels and, as they passed the crown, they distinctly heard the members of the family in front of them hissing at it. The room was incredibly dark, with bright lights shining on the crowns, orbs and sceptres behind the glass, so it was difficult to see who exactly was hissing, but there were enough different hisses to think the whole group was hissing. After they left the darkness and were back outside under the cloudy skies, Zoe broached the subject with her usual tact.

"Why were those ladies hissing at the crown?"

Uncle Reggie thought for a while about how to answer the question in a way that she would understand. "Hundreds of years ago there was a huge diamond which was found in a mine in what is now India. Over the years it was included in war booty as one or other empire fought over parts of that area, parts which are now in the current countries of India, Pakistan and Afghanistan. Each of those countries now thinks that they have a good claim on the diamond. Britain was "gifted" it, but there are some reservations on the legality of that gifting. The British put the diamond into their crown, so those ladies were expressing their disagreement with the British ownership of it."

"But can't they figure out who owns it?"

"Like everything, it's never black and white. If one army beats another and loots a city, is the loot legally now the property of the victor? If you legally buy something which is illegally gained, do you now legally own it? If an item changes hands under a different country's laws prior to you getting hold of it and there are disputes under that other country's laws about the previous transfer, where does that put your claim?"

"Is it worth much?"

"Well, for a while it was the biggest diamond known. They said that if a strong man threw a stone in each direction including upwards, and the space outlined by the distance those stones travelled was filled with gold and gems, then they would not be worth as much as the diamond. And that's not even counting the symbolic value to whoever holds it."

"Can't they just share it?"

"Maybe. It might be hard to persuade people to do that. It might set a precedent, and then everyone would want their stuff back." He guffawed. "One member of government once used the argument that they can't give everything back that they've pinched over time or else the British Museum would be empty."

They headed up the hill to the Underground station at Tower Hill. At the higher elevation, they could see that the clouds had darkened significantly, threatening rain. Marcus felt the first drops as they entered the station. They headed down on the escalators to the platform to wait for the train. There weren't many other people on the platform waiting with them, and when the train came it was eerily quiet. Not many people at all.

Each of the other platforms they passed on their way to Victoria were likewise devoid of passengers and the train was just pulling into Embankment when Marcus finally saw some people on the platforms. They were carrying placards and were making their way in fits and starts towards the train accompanied by yelling and shouts of rage and alarm. Looking out the window with mouth agape, Marcus watched as the group came closer, some of them with blood on their clothes and bleeding from wounds on their faces. In the background a second group—this time of policemen—emerged from the base of the stairs and ran after them. The doors of the train closed quickly before the fleeing protestors could get aboard and the train continued on its journey. Beside him Zoe was entrancing Uncle Reggie and Meredith with another of her fascinating stories, all three of them seemed oblivious to what was going on out the window.

Westminster and St James's Park were the only stops between Embankment and Victoria and each platform was entirely empty. The train didn't even stop at either station, just slowing slightly while out in the light before plunging back into the darkness of the tunnel. Marcus was still in disbelief at what he'd seen at Embankment. By the time he thought to ask Uncle Reggie and Aunt Meredith about it, they had arrived at Victoria Station.

They emerged from the Circle Line at Victoria Station, riding the various escalators to street level before continuing on into the station and finding the next train to take them back to the Manor. On the way back, as the rain closed in, Uncle Reggie got out his phone and arranged for them to be picked up from the train station at East Felstead. Marcus was relieved to be away from the crowds, excited by the things he'd finally seen in person, and exhausted by all the walking. He was also more than a little troubled by the suggestion of violence they'd experienced on the way home. He could see that Zoe was starting to fade, and was glad when they finally pulled into their destination to see William waiting in the Land Rover for them. When they arrived home, they had just walked through the door when Francine bustled over to them, concern written all over her face.

"Oh! I saw the news, are you ok?"

Uncle Reggie looked at Aunt Meredith who looked at Marcus in confusion. "Uh... yes, we're fine."

"They said that some of the protests turned violent and the riot police were called out. I was so worried!"

"Oh, dear! Well, we didn't see any of that," continued Aunt Meredith. "We saw the protests, but they were well behaved while we were there." Marcus nodded to himself. It looked like Uncle Reggie and Aunt Meredith had indeed been distracted by Zoe and hadn't seen any evidence of the violence.

"Ah, good," responded Francine, turning to walk back to her kitchen. "You hear rumours, is all..."

THE ESTATE

The next day dawned brightly, the overnight rain creating a layer of mist over the ground as it evaporated in the morning sun. There was still a slight chill under the cloudless sky but this promised to dissipate as the windless day progressed. Zoe and Marcus were breakfasting in the kitchen, chatting with Francine about all the things they'd seen the previous day, when Uncle Reggie and Aunty Meredith came into the room, hair still wet from their morning swim. As they prepared their cereal with fruit, Aunty Meredith casually asked Zoe what she planned on doing today. She couldn't keep the smile from her face when she asked so Zoe very quickly put one and one together.

"Riding?"

Aunty Meredith nodded and told her that the Equestrian Centre's manager, Molly, was expecting her at 10 am.

"Squeeeeee!" said Zoe, looking delighted.

"What about you, Marcus? What do you feel like doing?" Uncle Reggie asked.

"Oh, I thought I'd have a look around the estate, if that's ok?" Marcus responded. "The grounds are huge!"

"Sounds good," agreed Uncle Reggie.

After a quick brush of his teeth, Marcus walked out along the semi-circular driveway which connected the house to the country lane nearby. The estate was sprawling, but the lack of a huge gate like Buckingham Palace and a driveway up to the house across a perfectly cut lawn rather let the image down, Marcus thought, smiling to himself. As he reached the other end of the semi-circular driveway he noticed that there was in fact a wrought iron gate blocking the driveway, about as tall as he was and held up by two stone pillars with the name of the estate emblazoned on them. He continued along the lane, knowing that he was walking along the eastern edge of the property. Ahead of him he knew from the map that there would be a crossroads at the main road which was at the south eastern corner of the estate. The lane had slight curves and undulations which made it impossible to see the crossroads and was lined on both sides by mature trees which joined above forming a cosy canopy.

There was a break in the screen of trees to his right and a farm gate with "Warning" and "Private Property" signs led to a track which disappeared into the woods. There was a gap beside the post holding the padlocked gate in place meaning it was probably there to restrict cars rather than pedestrians, so Marcus slipped through and made his way beyond. The dirt track continued on, the trees on each side retreating until their tops no longer touched and a clearing of sorts turned into a carpark on his left. On the other side of the car park was a show jumping paddock, with an assortment of jumps and brightly coloured barrels. The path carried on, so Marcus continued his wandering. Ahead he saw another carpark, this one with a low-slung shed which, on closer inspection, turned out to be more of a hut.

He moved over to the hut and found out it was an Angling Club's members room. Leaflets and notices were pinned onto a sheltered noticeboard, alongside signs forbidding unauthorised fishing. Marcus got a little closer and found that there were some phone numbers for prospective members to call and a notification that night fishing would be starting back up in the summer. There were a couple of cars in the carpark and as he finished reading the notices a small man got out of one of the cars and came over with an anxious look on his face. Marcus guessed that he was an accountant. He had no way of knowing, of course, but the man looked the epitome of Marcus's view of an accountant. He was short, of average build, dressed in slacks and a wore business shirt under a green woollen sweater. He peered through thick glasses as he approached Marcus and asked if he could be of help. Marcus responded that he was just looking around, adding that his uncle was Reggie. The accountant looked relieved and told him that if he wanted to know anything at all about the angling club just to let him know. Marcus smiled and nodded, saying that he would, and continued on along the path. The lake sprawled to his left, a finger of land poking in towards the centre of it. A man on this finger of land had just got to his feet from a folding chair, the tautness of the fishing line in his hand showing that he'd just hooked a fish. Marcus paused and watched the angler wrestle with the fish, eventually landing a specimen about half the size of Marcus' arm span. Marcus smiled, somehow feeling he'd shared in the angler's success by watching him, and headed further into the woods.

He could just make out the road through the trees on the other side of the woods. The traffic was infrequent enough that it was easy to forget how close the lake was to the roadside, but if you ran a car off the road it could easily end up in the water.

The path left the clearing that included the car park on the edge of the fishing lake and headed into a wood with widely spaced mature trees. A pile of old horse dung indicated that this track was used by the Equestrian Centre and Marcus could see how the peaceful forest setting would make for an enjoyable ride. Past the trees on his right, he could see a pasture gleaming green in the sun, separated from the wood by a thin hedge. He wandered over and looked out over the field, which was empty of any animals, as was its neighbour, though by two giant old trees stood in the middle of the neighbouring pasture. Great shade for the sheep supposed Marcus.

He returned to the path and continued on through the forest, following a meandering trail, and sometime later found himself at a gate at the end of the track, leading on to a country lane. He'd enjoyed the walk, with just the birds in the trees for company, and the sun not yet too hot both because of the early hour and the canopy of leaves above.

He looked at his watch. About an hour. He contemplated taking the country lane the short distance to the main road and heading into East Felstead to have a look around town, but he was curious to discover more of his uncle's estate. He really couldn't figure out how Uncle Reggie had managed to get such an impressive spread of land. And the businesses! All food-related. That he could believe. Uncle Reggie was known for having a sweet tooth and a healthy appetite, but less known for business nous or even being good with money. His story about how he'd managed to become wealthy sounded fantastical, but what alternative better than any of the suggestions the extended family had come up with was there? Maybe Aunty Meredith had something to do with it? Shrugging to himself, he climbed the gate and headed up the country lane, keeping an eye out on the left-hand side of the road for the access gate to the unexplored half of the estate. This was the central piece of the figure eight, a narrow road joining the main road which ran along the southern border of the estate.

The slightly wonky left-hand oval of the estate melted along the hill, deeply and uniformly forested from Marcus's viewpoint, although he knew there must be clearings closer to the north-western corner where the fish farm and apiary were. The chicken farm overlooking the Earl's land had looked to be in a large pasture, so there would have to be another clearing next to the central lane of reasonable size. He realised that he should have paid more attention to the names of the roads which bordered the estate and with a shrug decided that he would give them names of his own. The road that ran along the northern border of the estate, along the top of the hill he considered in his head to be Crest Road or maybe North Boundary Road. Crest Road sounded best he thought, until he could find the map again. The road, or more accurately, country lane which bisected the two parts of the estate he decided to call Split Lane. The road which formed the southern border of the estate he decided to call Lake Road, in honour of the fishing lake nestled in beside it. Finally, the road forming the eastern border of the estate with the short driveway to the manor house he rather unimaginatively called Manor Road. He didn't know if there was a road along the westernmost border of the estate but suspected that he'd end up calling it West Road if there was.

He didn't have to walk far up Split Lane before he saw an open gate on the left-hand side which must be the starting point of the western part of the estate. Ahead of him, Split Lane continued along the flat, zig-zagging through a copse of trees before eventually running up the hill to the intersection with Crest Road. Just visible above the canopy of trees were the buildings of the chicken farm, nestled in the corner between Split Lane and Crest Road. Except for a short strip of clearing along the left-hand side of Split Lane, the rest of the left-hand side of the estate looked to be very heavily wooded.

He took the path through the gate and entered the woods. Eventually, the path popped out from the tree cover and he could see the sky above again. Here the ground started up the incline to the northern crest. To his left, a powerline took thick power cables up a slightly steeper hill to a pylon standing proudly, its winking red light warning planes away. The trees along the path that the powerlines took had been cleared, leaving the hillside cratered with just tufts of grass and ferns scattered across the exposed dirt. He could see buildings under the pylon at the top of the hill and wondered if those were the apiary and fish farm, so he chose to scramble up the uneven surface to the top of the hill. He had images of huge round tanks of water set into the ground with staff standing around with nets, scooping out metre-long fish into ice-filled bins.

There was a strip of lawn between the treeline and the fence on three sides of the square of plant and equipment, and Marcus could now see that the fence enclosed section where the power lines disappeared into was actually filled with plant and equipment while the low-slung buildings were separated from the fenced-in area by a white concrete driveway which left the compound to the north, its progress obscured by the woods.

The place had the feel of industrial complexes in movies and on TV where the hero breaks in, Marcus decided. It made him wonder if he had missed a "Do not Enter/Verboten!!" sign somewhere by choosing to climb the hill through the forest following the powerlines. If he was in fact trespassing, he should probably get away before anyone saw him. On the other hand, you would have thought the signage would have been better if that was the case, so he could always use that as an excuse.

He decided to follow the white concrete driveway out of the complex, and he'd no sooner reached the first corner when his vantage point made it clear where he was in comparison to the rest of the estate. The corner was the first bend in a dogleg that the driveway took before reaching the road which ran along the crest of the hill on the northern edge of the estate. Along the left-hand side of the driveway were more trees and on the right-hand side another pasture which led up to the road. The second bend of the dogleg driveway held a surprise which only became apparent when Marcus got closer. Nestled there was a gate, with a sizable cattlestop grid on both sides. The cattlestop consisted of a series of metal bars across a hole and was so-called because cars could drive across the top of the bars whereas cattle and other animals would not be able to pass. Marcus had never seen them this size though. This was two or three times the size of ones he'd seen on farms back home. He'd have to ask Uncle Reggie about it when he saw him next.

From the gate he could see into a square pasture, maybe 200 metres along each side. Each side was lined with tall trees, with the exception of about half the length of the northernmost edge, the one furthest away from the electrical plant. That part had a gap in the trees beyond which Marcus could see evidence of a track. While there were no trees, the track was bordered on both sides by a hip-high hedgerow. The pasture was not empty, not by a long shot. The white concrete continued on after the cattlestop, making an oval ring, well within the edges of the pasture and within that oval was a complex of what Marcus thought were buildings but as he got closer could see they were shipping containers—painted to appear more stylish, but shipping containers nonetheless.

On the northern side of the pasture, containers were stacked six on top of six, with an odd extra one on the bottom at the western end. They were painted white with stylish aqua trim along the edges which made them appear to be four groups of three containers each.

Running across the bottom of those on the south side, separated by two arm spans, was another white and aqua container, joined to the first and fourth of the container complex on both the ground and higher level by pipes—four single hand-span wide pipes disappearing into the same part of the widthwise container.

On the other side of the widthwise container (the south side) was another container, this one meagrely painted with a single coat of paint through which the shipping company logo was still faintly visible. An oversized garden shed perched on top of the white and aqua container complex, a square not much wider than one container width, with a collection of what appeared to be dolls houses made from natural unpainted wood on top of it.

Connecting the fronts of the container complex on the south side was a series of metal gangways that went as far as the garden shed on top, so three storeys in total—ground, first floor and second floor. There was certainly activity around, but at a very languid pace. Four men in white overalls were going about their business. One of them saw him and came over. He was a little bit taller than Marcus and about twenty years old. He had enough hair for two people, but it was not long. Instead, a fringe of never-ending curls covered the eye on one side of his face.

"Hey, man, what can I help you with?" he started, friendly enough.

"Oh, my Uncle Reggie owns the estate and I'm just having a look around," responded Marcus.

The guy frowned slightly and then smiled. "That's a new one," he said. "Let me check your story. What did you say your name was?"

"Marcus," said Marcus.

The guy's phone was already out and he talked quietly into it, never taking his eyes off Marcus. After a few minutes, he held the phone to his chest and told Marcus that his boss was just making a call. Not long after that, his boss came back onto the call and he went into listening mode again. Again he kept an eye on Marcus but this time he was checking off elements of Marcus' physical description. He smirked at one or other of what he was told over the phone and nodded, saying goodbye and then turning back to Marcus.

"You check out, I'll show you around. I'm Graham by the way." They shook hands. "Welcome to the Eastwell Estate Farm," Graham said, gesturing expansively. He pointed out the container complex. "There we have four fisheries, each taking three shipping containers each. They have twenty thousand fish in each of them and a thousand come to maturity for culling each month. The machinery in each fishery constantly cleans the water, taking out the fish sludge and putting the clean water back into circulation. The fish sludge runs out of those four pipes into this other shipping container here, where it's placed into the sealed system which bakes it and converts it into a dry fertiliser. We bag it and sell it, some of it goes into the gardens up at the manor house and some of it gets used here. Each day we take out the biggest fifty fish from each fishery and take them to the processing plant..."—here he pointed out the extra ground level container, the seventh on the bottom level—"where there is an automatic scaler, gutter and filleting machine. The results are perfectly prepared bream and sea bass fillets ready for the local restaurants and speciality stores, plus about twenty kilos of the most foul-smelling fish guts you can imagine. They're still trying to figure out a way to make money off the fish guts. There's not enough of it to justify a machine to extract the oil or convert it into fish food, plus you're not allowed to feed your fish any food made from themselves, so at the moment we give it away to farmers in the neighbourhood. James," he indicated one of the other white overall-wearing workers, "thinks it's a goodwill gesture, but I think they just wanted to get rid of the smell."

He paused here for breath, before indicating the very top of the container complex. "The garden shed thing up there," he started, "is one of our honey production sites. We have them dotted around the farms in the area. It's a lockable garden shed. Inside are a ladder and some empty plastic drums. There's also a hatch in the ceiling, which swings down. So you open the lock and climb up the ladder and then you're on the roof. The roof has sensors, so figures out someone is on it and sends a message to the manor house. If no one is supposed to be there then it raises an alarm. There's a bunch of special hives on the roof. Each one is hooked up to the computer in the shed. Inside each hive is a tiny camera that looks at the end of each comb in the hive. Once it looks like it's capped, it automatically realigns the comb so the honey flows into the drum that's in the garden shed. Once all the honey is out of the comb it realigns again, allowing the bees to start repopulating it. So you don't need to take the frame out to see if it's capped and you don't need to mess with the bees when you extract the honey either."

Marcus frowned. "I've seen documentaries on bees," he started. "The bees crawl all over the inside, so how are you going to get a good look at the bits to see if they are capped or not?"

Graham smiled. "I asked the same question," he said. "The camera doesn't take one shot - it's hooked up to the computer and it's constantly having a look - stitching together all the partial glimpses it takes of the comb until it builds up a single view, and then it decides how many of the cells are capped. All we do is rock up once a month in summer and swap out the drum."

Marcus nodded slowly, trying to find the flaw in the system. It seemed that they'd managed to take the danger out of honey production. "What's with the pole on top?"

Graham followed his finger and then nodded. "The pole in the middle holds a bunch of things. It's got the aerial so that the computer can communicate with head office and get the internet. It's also got a light on the pole so people know where the end of the pole is and don't accidentally damage it. Plus, it has some motion-detecting lights and a security camera in it so if anyone does climb up we can get a view of their faces."

Seeing the frowning look on Marcus's face, Graham continued upon. "Honey and the hives are really easy to steal," he continued. "The honey obviously you can sell, but there's even a black market for the hives, these ones especially. Every theft prevention thing we do is because someone tried to steal a honey station. We've taken to placing the stations up trees or other places equally difficult to get to. We get asked to install them all over the place—the farmers need the bees to pollinate their crops, so it's almost passive income—in summer and spring at least. You get an alert from head office, turn up and collect the honey, lock up afterwards and you're away—no bee suits, no getting stung, it's perfect. In winter the system monitors the health of the hive and occasionally we'll have to go out with some bread-like stuff and feed them to get them through the winter. Oh, and sometimes there's a swarm, but James is a proper beekeeper and he takes care of that."

"Sounds awesome," said Marcus. "So you don't need a centrifuge or anything fancy to get the honey out, it just flows out right away?"

"Science!" grinned Graham.

"So if the top shed is the bees, and the other fourteen containers are the fishery, what's the..."

"What's in the shitty container?" finished Graham. He let the question hang, before answering finally. "Red Gold."

Marcus looked at him for a second, trying to see if he was joking. "What do you mean, 'red gold'?"

"C'mon, let's have a look," said Graham, leading the way. He walked over to the last container, the badly painted one and unlocked a thick padlock on the door. Swinging it open he stepped back so that Marcus could look inside.

A corridor down the left-hand side of the container led all the way to the back. On the right-hand side were fourteen bays. Each bay had eight trays of plants in the front and nine trays behind them and Marcus could see that the trays were on a pulley system which meant you could rotate which of the seventeen trays you were looking at, similar to a ferris wheel. There really should have been eighteen, but there was a gap that allowed anyone standing in front of the bay to tend to the plants in front of them. The plants themselves were spread out on the tray with about twenty of them on each. They weren't flowering and just had a stubby growth sticking out of the ground. Marcus had no idea what he was looking at.

"I have no idea what I am looking at," he told Graham.

"Saffron," responded Graham. "The most expensive spice there is. It takes fifty flowers to make a gram of the spice and you have to harvest them by hand. It's ridiculous. With this set up we can make the harvesting as simple as possible and lock up the container for the downtime."

"Downtime?"

"Yeah, so you water the plants a little in spring, but that's all you have to do until October when they flower. Then you harvest them, lock the door and come back in spring again. Really low maintenance and very high margin crop."

"So, you pick the flowers, sell them, and that's it?"

"Heh, nah. There are three strings coming out of each flower. Red in colour, about the length of your little finger. Very, very thin though. So you sit there with tweezers—literally tweezers—and pluck each of them off the flower and put them in a container. When you're done, you empty the container into an oven for drying and then they turn to a powder which you put in little jars and sell to the local restaurants or as far away as the upmarket supermarkets in London. For 75 quid a bottle."

"And how much do you get in a bottle?"

"Two grams."

"Wow! How do they stop theft?"

"There are cameras in the container, but the cattlestop is there specially for the saffron."

Marcus looked confused.

"Not long after we sold our first bunch of saffron some likely-looking lads decided to steal the whole container. So they turned up in a big rig with a flatbed and a crane, ready to hook it up and steal it. They didn't realise your uncle had rigged the cattlestop. Unless you unlock it, the metal bars across the gap on one side give way under the weight of a truck. So the truck pulls up in the middle of the night, they cut the padlock on the gate and drive in. If they'd had a car or a van they would have driven straight in, but because they are in a truck they get halfway and then the bars on the right give way and the whole truck and trailer go over on their side. The guys jump out and run away, but it's pretty easy to track them down through the truck. They'd 'borrowed' it off a friend who was absolutely livid that it had been halfway wrecked. Their friend gave evidence against them and they were convicted."

"It sounds like everything is in danger of being stolen - the saffron, the honey…"

"Your uncle seemed to be paranoid, but we've had almost every attempt foiled so far. It's almost as if he expected someone to try to take everything away from him." Marcus thought back to the neighbourhood he and his uncle had grown up in and had to agree with that diagnosis.

"So how many people work here?" Marcus asked, looking around.

"We've run with as few as three, but when someone is on holiday and another one gets sick it's a bit much for one person in the Spring and Summer, what with the honey harvesting. So we have five on and that gives us time to do maintenance and preventative work during the winter. On the odd occasion in late winter when we're on top of everything we might have to go into the woodlands and maintain some tracks. You have to have cover because the fish have to be fed every day. We go through about 30kg of feed per fishery, so the last thing you want is to starve them to death because one person is in Tenerife and two have a cold."

"Sounds like it would be easy to goof off," said Marcus without thinking.

Graham looked shocked. "I guess it would be, but nobody would. Look, there aren't that many jobs out here in the country. Most of the local farmers bring in seasonal workers for their harvests because they will work for less and don't have to keep them on year-round. Your uncle pays better than minimum wage which is all everyone else around here will give you. And most other employers around here do zero-hour contracts..." Marcus started to ask what that was, but Graham answered pre-emptively "...that's when they only give you as many hours as they need you for, so no guarantee of work. No good if you have a mortgage, right? So if anyone goofs off then they get managed out and they give the job to someone who actually wants to work. There's actually a waiting list, so they don't even have to advertise."

Marcus nodded sagely.

When no further questions were forthcoming, Graham asked if Marcus would like to see the fish being fed.

"Sure!" he replied, and so they headed up the metal staircase up the side of the container complex to the gangways across the face of the containers. There were only doors on the first and second of each group of three containers, the pipe of fish sludge poking through the wall beside the door on the first container at about chest height before taking its apparently foul-smelling cargo to the processing container below. Graham opened the door in the second container and led him inside.

The interior walls of the containers on either side had been cut to make a single room of the three containers. The section that they stood in was about half the length of the container and empty save for the neatly stacked bags of pellets against the tank wall. The tank holding the fish formed an L shape, taking up the back half of the first and second containers and almost all of the third container. Machinery and tanks covered the first half of the first container. Marcus headed to the tank and looked over the edge. He was expecting it to be glass so was surprised that the walls of were steel plates, lined with blue plastic. The walls were about chest high and he could see that there were nets dividing the tank into three sections, each holding a shoal of fish. The first netted section held fish the length of his finger. In the next they were the size of his hand and in the last they were the length of his forearm. Behind him he heard Graham wrestling with a bag of feed. The top of the bag ripped off easily with string that was ingeniously woven through the end of the bag. He plunged a plastic container into the fish food pellets, stood up and sprayed them (they were each about the size of a fingertip) onto the water in the first section. The surface immediately came alive as the smallest of the fish went into a feeding frenzy.

"Do you want a go?" he asked Marcus, handing over the plastic container.

Half an hour later Marcus said his farewells and returned to his meanderings, leaving via the cattlestop and trying to see how it worked. There was no indication from his vantage point of the workings of the mechanism—the only thing he really noticed was that the gap beneath the metal bars was a lot deeper than he'd seen on farms. Now that he knew what to look for, he could see evidence of truck tipping: divots taken out of the earth, cracked branches, that sort of thing. He could only imagine how irate it must make the truck owners.

A few metres from the gate to Container Pasture was another gate, this one leading to Crest Road. Marcus decided not to explore the Laser Tag and Paintball that had been discussed, but instead to follow this new lane, knowing that it would lead to his Uncle and Aunt's cottage and the northwestern edge of the estate. He just had to call this one Cottage Lane. The lane started off in the open, the lower hedgerow making it easy to see the fields on either side, but very soon it dived into the woods, and not long after that Marcus came across the cottage.

It was a simple two-storey house, with what was once a detached garage now joined to the main house by a glass-panelled conservatory. The grass on the driveway was overgrown. Clumps of mossy matter collected and disposed of in one corner or another of the flower bed which ran along the base of the external brick wall suggested the gutters had recently been cleaned. Marcus knocked on the door to see if anyone was home—not because he particularly wanted to look around their cottage, but because he thought it would be seen as rude if he didn't.

He was a little relieved when nobody came to attend to his knocking, and just so that he'd be seen to have taken every step to alert them to his presence, he decided to dial his Uncle on the cell phone he'd been given.

"Hey Marcus," his uncle started, "everything ok?"

"Yeah, I've gone for a wander and am at the cottage. Nobody is answering, are you or Aunty Meredith here?"

"Ah, Meredith mentioned she might have to nip into town and I'm at the house, so if nobody's there, you're out of luck... Hang on... Francine's asking if you're coming back for lunch. There's left-over leek soup if you're keen. She serves it in these little loaves of bread. She scoops out the insides and pours the soup in and then grates some cheese on top so that the heat of the soup melts the cheese."

"That does sound awesome. I don't know how long it'll take me to get back but yeah, save me one of those!"

He suddenly realised that he was quite hungry. The phone told him it was after 1pm, so no wonder! He said goodbye to his uncle and paused while deciding which way to go back.

The land to the north of the cottage was a large expanse of natural flowers and grasses, hip high in parts. It was unusual to see so much usable land reverting back to nature. The land on the estate was mainly farm-ready—just add animals. But this was... different. Marcus shrugged. He guessed this meadow had been left for the bees that flitted from flower to flower and whatever rummaged through the long grass.

Cottage Lane terminated at the car park in front of the cottage, though Marcus could see a trail leading into the woods to the south. Marcus knew that the woodlands would eventually lead him to The Belt—that section of the estate between the left and right loops separated by Split Lane that he'd crossed earlier. Shrugging to himself, he headed off south, preferring the unknown wilderness over the path just travelled, even if it meant he might have to double back on himself should the going prove impossible.

The wall of trees behind the cottage turned out to have a turnstile over the three-wire fence which led directly into the forest. Rather than an impassable jungle to be hacked through with machete, it was a forest with a high canopy and very little underbrush. In fact, the floor of the forest was littered with a carpet of blue flowers—sometimes a threadbare carpet admittedly, as here and there the hollows or terrain precluded a consistent coverage and the rugged earth poked through.

He was marvelling at the beauty as he strode purposefully in the vague direction of The Belt when a flash of movement in the corner of his eye attracted his attention. About a hundred metres away, a fox had darted under a log, eyeing him warily. Marcus froze. It was only the size of a large cat or a small dog, so he didn't see it as a threat. He didn't know if he should be scared of the fox, so he just held its gaze until it decided to break off the staring contest and disappear back into the forest.

The odd root presented a trip risk, a patch of moss might hide a hole, but by and large he and nature got on ok and he enjoyed the fresh air and peace. He spied a lake ahead, smaller and more intimate than the fishing lake he'd seen earlier, and was startled to see a deer drinking at the edge. Another deer looked on in the distance, sniffed the air and then they both sprinted off. Marcus sniffed himself but couldn't see what was so offensive and continued on his way.

The undergrowth started to thicken up—more branches on the ground, vines threaded between the tree trunks and the odd fallen tree making navigation more interesting—but it wasn't long before he came across the path he'd taken earlier in the day. Following this back led him to The Belt and Split Lane, and instead of following his original path that had twisted and turned through the farm, he went directly across The Belt and followed a track which led a more direct route back to the manor house. It turned out to be a wooded path with open pasture on both sides, the fields on the left belonging to the neighbours, the ones on the right sometimes filled with cows or sheep.

By approaching the house in this direction, Marcus came across the lake in front of the house from a different angle. He stood there for a moment, marvelling at the contrast between the white of the house and the green of the hills and trees and lawn, along with the blue of the reflected sky in the lake. The contrasts continued: the other lakes he'd seen had been the fishing lake with the canopy of trees partly covering it and the one with the deer which had been totally under cover of the surrounding trees. The lake in front of the house had trees running all the way around the edge, but was totally exposed to the air.

Francine's soup loaves were waiting for him so he set off back to the house at an increased pace. When he arrived, there was the usual bustle of activity in the kitchen as she heated it up and he elected to sit outside and eat while looking at the lake from this side. The day was starting to look quite delightful, with only a light smattering of cloud spoiling an otherwise unblemished sky. Out of the corner of his eye he spied the twitching of a curtain from the room where he'd met the patient. When he turned to look more closely the movement stopped. Shrugging, he returned to his soup. It was really good, and the molten cheese on top was inspired. He was kind of glad Zoe wasn't there—she would have tried to eat the loaf first, working her way down until the soup would threaten to overflow, delighting in tempting chaos.

He was so engrossed in his soup that he didn't notice an attractive girl perhaps four years older than him approach with a quizzical look in her eye and a cup of coffee in her hand. She was dressed in jeans with a collared T-shirt monogrammed with the name of the estate on it.

"Hello, are you a guest here?" she asked.

Marcus hurriedly finished his mouthful of soup and cheese-laden bread to answer. "No, not a guest. Uncle Reggie is my..."

"Uncle?" she finished for him, smiling at his awkwardness. She had a heart-shaped face with a button nose, dimples when she smiled and a bob haircut. Marcus stared.

"Ah, that makes sense," she said, ignoring the stare and casting her eyes over the estate. "We've only got the one guest and I've already made up her room for the day, so..." she trailed off.

Marcus wanted to keep her talking. "So, you work here?" he managed.

She looked at the logo on her shirt and smiled wryly. "What gave it away? Yeah, my name's Marie. I clean and make up rooms and when there's an event at the hall I wander through the people in their fancy dresses and hand out glasses of champagne."

Marcus racked his brain for something smart to say. "So what do you do when there's only one guest in the whole place?"

Marie looked serious. "Oh, I chat with Uncle Reggie's nephew, have a cup of coffee and a smoke, and stare out across the lake." She broke into a smile. "Nah, they find work for you. Sometimes it's gardening, sometimes it's maintenance work and sometimes, when they can't think of anything else, they get you to ride through the estate on the bridle paths and look for fences which need repairing or overgrowth that needs cutting back. Those are the best days."

Marcus realised he hadn't introduced himself. "Oh, I'm Marcus by the way." They shook hands. Marie noticed Marcus had finished his soup and pulled out a packet of cigarettes. "Do you mind?" she asked.

Marcus wouldn't have minded if she'd pulled out an ice pick and stuck him through the ear with it. "No, not at all," he said. She lit up, blowing the smoke up and away from him before casting a sideways glance at him. "So, are you going to take over the family business?" she asked, her casual body language belied by her steady gaze.

"Hmm, what now?" Marcus managed.

"'Uncle Reggie doesn't have any kids, right? And there's a few years left in him, but you're the first family member he's brought to the estate, so you must be the chosen one, right?"

"There are other nieces and nephews who are older than me—I'm not even the oldest in my family!"

"So why are you here, and not them? You must be the favourite."

"Oh! No, you see Uncle Reggie had this special air ticket that was expiring. It let two people travel if you just paid for the taxes. So me and Zoe had school holidays and Mum got Dad to pay for the taxes and here we are. Uncle Reggie certainly hasn't said anything." Uncle Reggie may not have said anything but Marcus' mother certainly had. Her parting words to him in the airport had been at high volume. "Be nice to your Uncle - he's loaded!" ringing around the cavernous Departures lounge. He felt a little uncomfortable, like he was an insect being examined by a scientist.

"The heir," she pronounced grandly. "The heir of Eastwell Manor.

Straight out of a Dickens novel."

Desperate to change the topic, just in case Uncle Reggie discovered Marcus' mother's ulterior plan for his visit from Marie, but wanting to keep talking with her, Marcus flailed around trying to think of alternative subjects. "So, tell me about the guest! Who is she?"

Marie seemed surprised. "I didn't say it was a she. How did you know it wasn't a man?"

"Plastic surgery, right?"

Marie snorted. "We get enough rich men through here, recuperating after a tummy tuck or eye lift. But yeah, you're right. She's apparently an actress. Wanting to break into the American market, so nose, eyes, tits, the usual."

Marcus nodded, affecting the air of a cynical man of the world, trying to make a connection by saying the right thing. "Yeah, terrible, you should be able to get by on just your talents," he said, trying to see her reaction, while simultaneously casting a world-weary look across the lawn towards the lake.

She wrinkled her nose. "Sure," she said. And Marcus couldn't tell if the wrinkle was in disgust, amusement or boredom. He changed tack.

"So what is there to do for fun around here?" he tried.

"Well, if you're interested in shooting people there's paintball and laser tag, but mainly we play pool and darts at The Duck's Bark. It's a gastropub. We're going tonight. Wednesday's are quieter. Just locals. You should come along. Anyways, back to the grindstone!" She finished her cigarette and took the butt and coffee cup inside with her.

Marcus watched her go. An invitation to the local—that was practically a date! He'd have to see if Uncle Reggie would take them all there for dinner.

THE DUCK'S BARK

Marcus was surprised that Uncle Reggie didn't seem to need much persuading that maybe tonight they should go to the Duck's Bark for dinner. He dressed it up in such a way to present it as such a famous gastropub that had come up in his research on things to do in the area and although he thought he saw a glimmer of a smile from Aunty Meredith he thought he'd done a good job hiding his real reasons. Uncle Reggie did seem somewhat distracted. While they were waiting he would occasionally stare out over the estate or gaze at his phone as if expecting someone to call.

William dropped the four of them off at the pub, a ten-minute drive from the house. The pub was a two-storey building, walls of off-white stucco, downstairs decorated with fake black columns holding up a plinth with the pub's name emblazoned proudly in all caps, bookmarked by an "Established 1839" at one end and a jaunty silhouette of a duck at the other. When they headed through the main doors to the bar, Marcus saw that the building was deceptively deep, a dining room adjacent to the main bar on one side of the entranceway, and the games room on the other. A staircase accessing both upper floors and the basement held signage pointing to the bathrooms. The walls were a dark stained wood, decorated with various farming implements and sepia pictures of farmers, horses and pastoral scenes. Dotted around the pub were stuffed ducks collecting dust.

As they headed into the dining room, Marcus casually glanced into the games room but nobody was there. Yet, he told himself. Nobody was in there yet. It was a little early after all. There were two men sitting in the corner at a table in the bar area, drinking beers from pint glasses and talking quietly among themselves, but apart from them and the barman, the place was quiet.

The barman welcomed Uncle Reggie warmly by name, nodding to Aunt Meredith and asking them if they would be having a drink or food, before leading them to a table very near the bar area and giving them four menus.

"Any drinks to start?" asked the bartender.

"Thanks Robert, I'll have a pint of your Special, what are you after, dear?"

Aunty Meredith ordered a white wine and Zoe got a lemonade.

"Can I get a pint of Special too," asked Marcus, wanting to show Marie how mature he was when she got there.

Robert the barman flicked a glance over at Uncle Reggie who nodded very slightly. "Well, the law says that if you're sixteen and with a parent or guardian, then you can have a drink with a meal, so that should be alright," and then he headed away behind the bar. Marcus kept his mouth shut. If Robert thought he was sixteen and that meant Marcus could have a beer, then he wasn't going to correct him. Besides there were only three months before his birthday, so it wasn't really much of a fib. By the time Robert brought over the drinks, they'd had enough time to figure out what they wanted. Uncle Reggie and Zoe had the Bark Burger while Marcus had the fish and chips and Aunt Meredith had the beetroot and pumpkin salad.

Robert disappeared out the back into the kitchen, coming back out as the door opened and two men came in. They were rough-looking, middle-aged, dressed in camouflage jackets and smelt of cigarette smoke. One had matching camouflage pants while the other had jeans. They sat in the bar area beside one another in a booth which overlooked both the restaurant's seated area as well as the other bar patrons. Robert greeted them a little coldly, thought Marcus, and served them their drinks. He returned to his station behind the bar and raised his voice a little to address Uncle Reggie.

"I hear you had a bit of a ruckus in the early hours this morning?" His voice was pitched to carry to their table, but it obviously was for the other occupants of the bar as well. Conversation had ceased at both of the other two tables in the bar. Nobody was making eye contact, but they were all listening.

"I guess you could say that." Uncle Reggie paused. "One of the prize fish was stolen from the lake."

"Stolen from the lake you say? That's terrible! What size would you say that would have been?"

"We reckon it was one of the twenty kilogram ones," replied Uncle Reggie. Marcus noticed that Aunt Meredith was paying close attention to the conversation as well, though she seemed to be more interested in the reactions of the newcomers.

"What would that be in pounds?" asked Robert.

"Probably close to forty-five pounds," allowed Uncle Reggie.

Robert whistled low and slow. "And what would that be worth? To the wicked men what stole it?"

"Probably close to thirty thousand pounds."

One of the newcomers frowned slightly at that and the other cast his eyes towards the ceiling, rubbing his face with one calloused and dirty hand.

"Quite the fish then! Lucky you had those cameras set up, isn't it?"

The guy with jeans glared angrily at his companion, who ducked his head and whispered under his breath in return.

"Oh yeah, we got some good footage of the guys, their car... and their address as well."

Robert was pointedly ignoring the newcomers, focussing his attention on Uncle Reggie, but did seem to be enjoying his central role in the theatre.

"About a hundred anglers caught that fish last year, so it'll be good to put the guys who stole him away."

The two newcomers pushed their chairs out and walked out of the bar, leaving their drinks on their table half finished. Robert winked at Uncle

Reggie and Uncle Reggie mimed tipping his cap in return.

"If those guys stole the fish, shouldn't you have called the Police? Won't they get away?" asked Marcus.

Aunt Meredith answered. "Uncle Reggie has already shared their details with the Police. The guy on the left was Guy Fenris and the one on the right was Tobias Goodacre. They're paying them a call early tomorrow."

"Won't they just run away? Not go home?"

"Those two? Nah, their whole lives are here. They've got extended family in the area, they're not the type to cut and run. They obviously hoped that fishing at night would be enough to hide what they were doing. But…"

"How did you get the address details? From the car registration?"

Uncle Reggie looked around to make sure nobody else was listening. "So kids, you know back home how you don't show off anything flash you've got?" They both nodded in response. "Well, it's a bit hard to do that over here when it's an estate and everybody can see your business." He leaned in and lowered his voice. "So I decided to invest in some… high tech surveillance," he continued.

"Like cameras? Night vision cameras?" Marcus guessed.

Uncle Reggie straightened, nodding a little before continuing. "Yeah it started with a few cameras - especially around the fishing lake. You've seen how close that is to the main road, right? But then I thought what would happen if someone wore a mask or covered their license plate? Having footage of someone stealing your stuff when you can't ID their face or car doesn't help anyone, right?"

Marcus frowned, not following. "Sure, so…?"

"So I invested a couple of grand in some drones," he said.

Aunt Meredith looked amused. "A couple!" she snorted.

"OK, it's a little more involved than that. Most of the money went into programming and battery technology. Basically there's a little fleet which can coordinate their movements and when the fixed cameras raise a silent alarm, the drones follow the 'people of interest'."

Marcus frowned. "My friend Talesi has a drone and it only lasts a half hour per battery."

Uncle Reggie nodded. "Yeah, that's about as long as mine lasts for as well. But I have four of them, and they take it in turns staying following the 'people of interest'. When their battery runs down, the next one takes over. As long as the people that they're following remain within a thirty mile radius of the docking station, then we can follow them. It's really hard case to watch. The drone on point follows at the speed of the people it's following. So on country roads that's about thirty miles an hour—call it fifty kilometres an hour. When the battery starts to get low the next drone comes online and absolutely zooms to catch up. The original drone then honks it back to the recharging station and lands on its landing pad, which is a recharging mat. I was watching during the demonstrations and you'd think they were alive. You know sheepdogs? They know what they have to do and they're focused on their job. It was like that—the narrow focus of the drone on the car it was following, and when the replacement came online it wasted no time getting to the replacement point. And then when it took over it went from eighty miles an hour back down to thirty and it felt like it was so disappointed that it had to go so slow to match the car's speed. But yeah, they can stay on station for a long time. This morning I looked at the footage and they'd followed our friend over there back to his house. He had no idea. Watched him get out of his car with the plastic crate with the fish in it. Will be really hard for him to talk his way out of this one."

Marcus took a long sip of his beer. And grimaced. He looked over at Uncle Reggie. He hadn't touched his beer and was watching Marcus. "Yeah, it's pretty bad, right?"

"Oh, no, I have beer all the time back home. This is just a little…"

"Different? Bitter? Hoppy?" Uncle Reggie smiled. "Yeah, the locals like it, so I do my bit and buy it when I can, to show support. But it's pretty bad. Stops me from getting drunk."

Marcus changed the subject. "Robert seems friendly."

Aunt Meredith snorted again. "He should—we get him to provide the drinks for the Christmas Party each year. All the staff and all their families come to the Hall up near the Equestrian Centre for a big meal. He makes more from that one party than the pub brings in all year!"

Marcus looked at his beer.

"It's not all Robert's Special," Meredith assured him.

Robert brought over the burgers with a generous amount of salad and fries filling the remainder of the plates. "Salad and fish and chips are on their way and I'll bring some ketchup and mayonnaise over too," he said. "Looks like you've avoided the rush," he mentioned as he departed, indicating with his chin that a new group had arrived. There were six of them. Marcus was surprised to see Graham was one of them and delighted to see that Marie was there too. They headed into the games room, one of the new arrivals that Marcus didn't know staying at the bar to order drinks. Robert called out that he'd be right there as he carried Meredith's salad and the fish and chips along with a plastic bottle of ketchup and mayonnaise under each arm to their table. Marcus hadn't eaten out at any posh restaurants but could tell that Robert's delivery style probably wasn't something that he'd see there if he had. Robert managed to get the plates onto the table without spilling anything and extricated the bottles of condiments without incident before heading back to the bar.

With a last look back towards the games room, Marcus turned his attention to the fish and chips, catching a meaningful glance passing between his Aunt and Uncle out of the corner of his eye. The topic of conversation turned to Zoe and her horse adventures and without much prompting she regaled them with the tales of mucking out the horses and learning how to put bridles and saddles and other equipment on them. Marcus listened with one ear, trying to figure out a way of breaking away from the dinner table and casually passing the games room.

Zoe didn't seem to have any end to the tales she wanted to tell about her adventures and what she wanted to do with the remainder of the holiday—show jumping and pony trekking through the woods featured strongly, in a bewildering array of variations and permutations. All the talking did slow down her eating though, so by the time the other three had finished, she still had a lot on her plate.

Marcus, on the other hand, had found his first beer pretty hard going. He'd had the odd beer with his Dad back home—more of a novelty and a bonding experience rather than a taste driven experience—and the plain lagers had been much easier to drink than the strange tasting brew in the tall glass that he was trying to get through here. He did notice that Uncle Reggie's glass hadn't gone down much either. Periodically a peal of raucous laughter emanated from the games room, and each time Marcus turned to see if he could discover what was going on.

Meredith and Uncle Reggie started to talk about the dinner at the neighbouring estate that they'd all be going to the following night. "The Earl invites us every year, and it's usually just after your Aunt's birthday. You guys just missed that. It was the Friday before you arrived."

"So is it a formal affair? I don't have a suit," worried Marcus.

"No, the invite said dress code casual, so you should be fine with jeans," said Aunty Meredith.

"The invite? An actual paper invite? Like for weddings and that?"

"Yeah, he does things properly, does our friend the Earl."

Just then, Robert came back over and collected their plates. "How was everything? Can I interest anyone in a dessert?"

Zoe had only just finished her burger and fries and was mopping up the last of the sauce on the plate as Robert had cleared it, but was definitely keen on dessert. Robert dropped off menus and disappeared back to the bar. Marcus had an idea. After a casual glance at the menu he put it down on the table and looked up.

"Actually, there's nothing on the menu that's grabbing me. Do you mind if I go and check out the games room? Graham, the guy I met today, is there and I want to say Hi."

Aunty Meredith and Uncle Reggie both smiled at him, Aunty Meredith waving him away. "Of course, go! Say hi! We'll share a dessert over here."

At the mention of sharing, Uncle Reggie's smile faltered, but he too made encouraging noises, and so Marcus headed into the games room, his three-quarter-full pint glass in hand.

Inside, Graham was lining up a shot on the pool table, watched by the five others, Marie in the middle of them all, chatting away amicably. Graham was the first to notice him, glancing up after following the trajectories of the balls across the table and breaking into a grin.

"Marcus!" he exclaimed, coming around the end of the table and approaching him with his hand extended. "Good to see you!"

Marcus hurriedly switched his beer to his left hand and shook Graham's hand.

"Come and meet everyone," he said, rattling off the names which went in one ear and out the other until he came to Marie... who he introduced as his girlfriend. Marcus' smile flickered as he realised that Marie had just been being friendly with her invite. She'd seemed genuine, so it wasn't like he'd been made fun of, but he still felt foolish.

"Sorry?"

"I said how long have you been in England?" one of the others asked.

Marcus thought about it. "I think we arrived Tuesday, so that would make it... three days?"

"And what do you think? Have you seen much?"

"It's great, we went into London and saw the Castle and the Palace. Apparently you used to be able to go inside. Not while the Queen was there, obviously."

"Yeah, they stopped doing that recently, after that incident with the Prince," said Peter, or was it Paul?

"What happened there? It covered the news for a while back home but nobody could tell what exactly happened."

Peter - definitely Peter - looked serious for a second before responding. "Someone just finally told him the truth when he was out doing a meet and greet in the countryside." There seemed to be some sort of dissent among his friends at his answer, the murmuring coalescing into one of the other girls, a bookish-looking redhead with freckles and oversized glasses perched on a button nose, leading the disagreeing.

"It was just rude what they did. They backed that poor man into a corner and went off their nut at him. He was just there to open the Community Centre and then some nutcase got up in his face."

"That 'nutcase' was just letting him know that he can't keep being a drain on society and that taking money from the public purse just makes him the equivalent of him being on benefits except he's getting thousands more than anyone else..."

"The Royal Family brings in more in tourism than they cost the public," interrupted one of the others. Marcus just watched as the vibe in the room twisted so suddenly, following the conversations like a spectator at a demented tennis match, his eyes widening as the temperature in the room rose.

"Let's just say that opinions differ on the matter," interjected Marie, walking over to Barry and taking the pool cue from his hand, "and talk about something else, shall we?" She potted a ball and then stalked to the other side of the table.

Marcus watched as she potted another ball before missing her next shot, the cue ball coming to rest against the cushion closest to him. She grimaced and handed the cue to Peter/Paul who lined up his shot. Graham leaned over to Marcus.

"Spot the Republicans, huh? Susan and Philip..."—so it was Philip, not Peter or Paul— "definitely don't like the Royal Family. Samantha's mum is staunchly supportive. She has all the tea towels and teaspoons with all the weddings and christening dates on them and follows them all in the magazines. Loves them."

Marie surveyed the group, focussing on their drinks. "Anyone else need a drink? Philip, you ok there? Sam? Marcus?" Marcus looked down at his glass, still half full, and shook his head no. Marie headed out to the bar just as Uncle Reggie came into the games room.

"Gidday Graham, how're things?"

"Good Reg, good. Just about to show Marcus here how it's done on the pool table—are you sticking around?"

"Nah, we have to get Zoe home in time for bed so she can go riding again tomorrow," Uncle Reggie said, and then, noticing the look on Marcus' face he continued, "but if you wanted to stay, that's cool."

Marcus allowed that it might indeed be cool to stay a little while longer. Uncle Reggie leaned closer and spoke softly. "You've got your phone, right? Charged? Cool. Don't let them talk you into anything you don't want to do. Don't get in a car with anyone who has been drinking. Do call me or William for a ride home at any time. At any time at all, right?" Marcus nodded. Uncle Reggie got out his wallet and handed him a note. "Oh, and here's £20, have fun."

"Are you on tomorrow?" Uncle Reggie asked Graham.

"Yeah, I'm on from 10," Graham replied.

"So I imagine you won't be out too late," suggested Uncle Reggie.

"Nah, just a few quiets," replied Graham. "We'll make sure he gets home ok."

"Cool, have fun all," Uncle Reggie called as he left the games room.

Marie came back with three beers—an awkward triangle, with each hand framing the glass on that side plus half the middle one. Her face was a picture of concentration and she bit her lip as she gently deposited the drinks on the table.

Samantha took a sip of hers and nodded her thanks. "Cheers. Hey, did you know Marcus knows Reggie?"

Marie smiled knowingly, turning towards Marcus. "Knows him? Marcus is his nephew!"

Samantha nodded appreciably. "Nice to come from money," she said, not unkindly.

Marcus frowned, thinking about his life thus far. "Oh, no. We're not rich," he managed.

Samantha pursed her lips and looked thoughtful. "So you're one of the proletariat, yet your uncle is one of the owners of the means of production?"

Marcus looked from face to face, trying to glean a clue as to what an acceptable answer might be. Or to what the question was in the first place. Marie chastised Samantha. "Stop giving him a hard time. It's not his fault his Uncle is rich." She turned her attention back to Marcus. "Sam sat in some courses at Uni and has some strong ideas. I'm not sure I understand all of them though."

Marcus frowned. If it wasn't his fault that his Uncle was rich, then was it any of the Royal Family's fault that their parents or grandparents or uncles or aunts were rich either? He quickly realised that bringing up this argument might provoke a contentious discussion and instead decided to focus on drinking his beer. By this time the beer was flat and warm and he decided he could probably try a different drink without causing offense, so headed to the bar.

Looking back on the evening afterwards, that was the latest memory of which he could be 100% sure, the remainder of the evening amounting to snippets and snatched portions of conversation, lengthy periods of watching other people talking, the odd game of pool where sometimes the balls refused to stay on the table and general laughter and camaraderie.

HANGOVER

The next morning Marcus woke late and stumbled into the shower. He felt terrible—a pulsing headache right behind his eyes and his mouth felt like it was full of cotton. He let the hot water run long, waiting for the dull thump in his temple to stop hurting so much. Eventually he got out and staggered back to his room. He was tempted to slither back into bed and curl up in a protective ball for the rest of the day, but he figured he'd feel better with some food in his stomach. If he could keep it down. He dressed slowly and carefully. As long as he kept upright he was ok. Bending over to do up his shoelaces sent the world spinning, but he managed to wait it out and sat on the bed to continue the task.

The climb down the stairs was twenty times longer than he remembered it and, as he approached the kitchen, the bustling noises of Francine cooking rang loudly in his ears. The noise ceased once he reached the doorway though, and they all stopped to look at him as he blinked in the brighter natural light streaming through the ample windows.

"Here he is," Uncle Reggie announced.

"How many eggs did you want?" asked Francine, loading a frying pan with bacon.

"Uhhhh..." managed Marcus. "What happened?"

"Well, good news and bad news, I guess," continued Uncle Reggie. "There was a mechanical problem with the fishery so Graham got an emergency call and had to get back to the tanks. You and the others kept going and without his guiding hand had a few too many. One of the others was going to drive you home but they too had had a little bit too much, so you got on your phone and tried to let us know you needed a lift. The powers of speech were a little beyond you by that time, but we got the gist. Robert had already let us know the situation, so we gave Samantha and Felix a lift home too. You're an entertaining drunk I must admit, though I didn't expect to hear a rant on communism! Oh and I think William has cleaned up last night's dinner. You got most of it out of the window."

Some fleeting images flashed back between painful stabs to Marcus' brain. He vaguely remembered conversations with Samantha and Felix and feeling a justified anger about something... the country lanes... needing fresh air... the window and then staggering up the stairs to his bedroom. Singing? Was there singing?

Francine placed the cooked breakfast in front of him and then slid a glass of orange juice with a little blister pack of pills alongside it with a wink. He found he was quite hungry, so washed down a pair of pain relief pills with a mouthful of orange juice before seeing to the bacon and eggs.

William swung past the door and Uncle Reggie called him in. "Could you take Marcus fishing this morning, William? It would be good for him to get some fresh air."

William seemed very taken with that idea and smiled his agreement. "I'll swing past in half an hour, Marcus. Give you time to clean your teeth and what not."

Half an hour later Marcus was strolling through the estate behind William who carried two fishing rods, a tackle box and a pair of folding chairs. He was now sporting an olive vest festooned with pockets and a wide brimmed hat decorated with hooks and lures. A light breeze pushed patchy clouds across an otherwise bright blue sky and whenever the sun poked out there was a brief moment where the hangover reminded him that it hadn't left just yet. Marcus had to speed up a little to keep up with William who seemed to be a man on a mission. They made quick work of the short walk and Marcus noticed that this time there wasn't anyone in the carpark or on the lake. Without pausing, William headed to the finger of land sticking out into the middle of the lake and unfolded the two chairs, placing them beside each other but facing opposite directions.

Marcus couldn't read William's mood. Was he pissed off that he had to clean up the car? That he'd been called out late last night? Had Marcus said something insulting last night? Was fishing a punishment for him? Why did he have his own fishing gear? Or did it belong to the estate? As William stood and assembled the fishing pole, Marcus decided to at least try to apologise.

"I'm sorry I made a mess of the car," he tried.

William looked surprised. "Oh, I'm not," he replied.

Marcus frowned, not understanding. "And sorry I called so late," he continued.

William smiled and shook his head. "Not at all. You know why?"

Marcus shook his head, gently because it hurt.

"Whenever your uncle gets me to do something unpleasant—getting up early, staying out late, cleaning vomit out of the car, that sort of thing, he gives me a couple of hours on the lake."

Marcus looked around at the lake. "Which you like?"

"I love the fishing," William interrupted. "It's calm and peaceful. Just you and the fish." William had sorted out Marcus's line for him and handed him the rod. "Do you know how to cast?" he asked.

Marcus shook his head. Again regretting it.

William showed Marcus how to get the lure into the water and how to wind it back afterwards. Marcus was surprised how quickly he picked it up and then sat in his chair, watching the float bob gently in what little current there was in the lake.

William also cast off and sat in his chair with a relaxed sigh. There followed about ten minutes of companionable silence, the breeze in the trees, the birds twittering and the odd car driving past were the only noises. The pills from breakfast must have kicked in because Marcus's head stopped throbbing and he started to feel a little more human.

"William, is Uncle Reggie a good boss?"

He could feel William eyeing him sidelong from behind the wide brim of his hat. "What makes you ask that?" he managed.

"Well, it seems to me that he gives a lot of people jobs and a Christmas party and the barman at the Duck's Bark seemed to like him. That must mean that everyone likes him. But those guys stole the fish... so..."

Marcus sensed William's internal conflict. Eventually it seemed he came to a conclusion and answered.

"Reggie gave us this job at a critical time in me and Francine's lives. There'd been a bit of a mixup with our pensions with a previous employer and we weren't looking at a particularly comfortable retirement which will be in a few years. The agreement with Reggie is very beneficial to us—room and board with enough to get by on, and a very generous contribution to our pension, meaning that when we do retire we'll be much better off than we thought we would be. Plus the work isn't hard and even when it is inconvenient or dirty there are benefits. So yes, your uncle and I get along fine. And you're right, he does employ a lot of locals. But no, not everyone likes him. Nobody likes the boss, right? If you're beholden to him for your job you resent him having power over you and if you aren't then you're jealous that he owns all those businesses. But people are nice enough to your face, you just can't tell what they're saying behind your back."

"That's terrible!"

"Nah, that's life. When I first started here he'd had the estate for a little over a year and you could tell he wanted people to like him. He went a bit overboard on the Christmas party, that sort of thing. But he realised that you can't buy people and they can sense when you're trying and hate you for it. So I think he's better now—it's taken a while but he just does his own thing and lets the managers run the businesses. Or maybe he just learned how to not give a shit."

Marcus was a little surprised that William was so talkative. He'd supposed that because he hadn't been very talkative at any of the other times he'd been around that he was one of the brooding silent types. Turns out you just needed a fishing line.

"Tell me about back home," said William after a while.

"What would you like to know?"

"Where do you live? What does your Dad do? What do you do for fun?"

Marcus thought about that for a while. "Well, the house we live in is a little run down. I'm lucky I have my own room now that my older brother has moved out. He stays with his girlfriend most of the time. But where we live isn't the best neighbourhood. Sometimes me and Zoe stay with our Grandmother instead, when Mum has a late shift. Our place is just a rental but it's a bit of a hole to tell you the truth."

"And what does your Dad do?"

"Oh, he works in a factory where they make PVC pipes. We see him maybe two weekends a month. And at Christmas and all the family events like birthdays and that sort of thing."

"So he's still around?"

"Yeah definitely."

"Are you still at school?"

"Yeah, we're halfway through the school year. I've got two more after this one."

"And what happens after that?"

"I don't know."

"Well, what do you want to happen?"

Marcus thought about it for a bit. He wondered if William would understand. "Sometimes I don't think it matters what I want."

William turned to look at him. "What do you mean?" he asked.

"Well, school is ok I guess, but not a lot of fun. And if I went to university, then I'd need to do another three years of school after high school, which is just more of the same really. But if I don't go to university I'll have to find a job and that sounds like a bit of a grind. So, nothing really appeals."

"What fifteen-year-old knows what he wants to do for the rest of his life?" William asked rhetorically. "But until you know where you want to go, you'll be aimlessly drifting along. The danger is that by the time you do figure out what you want to do, it'll be too late to get on that path. You can lose a lot of years that way."

Marcus grimaced. "I guess."

William hadn't finished. "Can I give you some advice? Freely given, so worth what you paid for it."

Marcus nodded.

"Try things. The reason you don't know what you want to do is because you haven't been exposed to it yet. So you have to try a whole bunch of things. And some of those things are only available at places like universities, so it may be that in order to try those things you have to go to university and then transfer to the thing which excites you."

Marcus nodded again. "I guess that makes sense."

William put a hand on his shoulder. "But when you figure out that thing you want to do, you have to go after it with both hands. You have to commit to getting it. Can you do that for me?"

Marcus thought that William was actually talking to the younger version of himself, rather than Marcus. "Yes, of course," he managed.

William returned to fishing.

"Isn't university expensive over in New Zealand? Over here going to university is very expensive."

"You can get loans and if you're lucky, maybe a scholarship."

"Oh, and the scholarship pays for everything, including living costs?"

"Oh, no. It's not like the American scholarships where they pay for everything. These ones give you maybe five hundred dollars. Something like that."

"Wow, so you still have to work hard to go then. Uncle Reggie wouldn't give you any money for school then?"

"Well, he hasn't given my brother any money that I know of, and he hasn't mentioned it to me, so I don't think so."

There was silence for a while, the two of them comfortable just staring in their different directions at the lake and the lines disappearing into the water. A ute drove by with a farm dog yapping from the back of it, the unexpected interruption accentuating the silence.

"Do you feel that?" asked William. "That sense of a moment? Like this minute stretched out across the day, with the sun shining off the lake and the silence and peace and quiet?"

"Yeah, I feel it," replied Marcus.

"Remember it, commit it to memory. When you're back home and if things ever get bad, with school or at home or wherever, remember this moment. And feel the peace, feel the clean air in your lungs and the birdsong in your ears. And use it to gain strength."

DINNER

Somehow the decision was made to walk to the dinner at the Earl's Manor. The moon was a night or two from being full, the weather was supposed to be fine, and the ground underfoot was dry, so Reggie, Meredith, Zoe and Marcus headed out along the tracks past the lake in front of the house to Split Lane. From there they headed north towards Crest Road, through the chicane in the lane surrounded by trees, and along the meadow on the left which held the chicken farm. The lane headed gently uphill from the chicane, the meadow being at an equal gradient, and as a result they had a great view over the countryside to the right of the lane through the lines of trees to Dormansland Manor. The country lanes didn't have street lights, but the moonlight shone brightly and the going was easy, so it took maybe only half an hour to reach the gates of the Manor.

An almost medieval looking house with a conical roof stood at the entrance to the driveway which continued on, bordered by thick hedges even taller than Uncle Reggie and a line of mature trees. It was much darker on the driveway than out in the open, the trees' canopy shading the moonlight. It made for eerie shadows and stunning effects when the moonlight streamed through the leaves. The driveway led onto an open green in front of the main house, an imposing three-storey brown brick building with a white entrance way. A triple garage on the right suggested more outbuildings beyond. Uncle Reggie walked up to the door and knocked.

The door opened and a butler appeared. "I didn't hear you pull up, do please come in."

"Oh, we walked," said Uncle Reggie as he led the way. They gathered in the hallway taking in the decor as the butler disappeared into the innards of the mansion. Whereas Eastwell was decorated haphazardly with modern fittings taking precedence over historical fixtures, the Earl's manor was a chaotic collision of many century's styles. Eastwell had a bulk purchase of classic watercolours on the walls, while Dormansland featured oversized oil portraits of stern family members attended by wives and hunting dogs. The wood was stained darker than at Eastwell and the lights didn't penetrate into every corner, giving Marcus the sensation that there was something interesting lurking just out of view. Before he could manoeuvre to get a better look to see if it was a suit of armour or some unfortunate family member shackled in the corner, the butler returned trailing an imperious, middle-aged man topped with a coiffe of blonde hair with the sides shaved close. A very well-kept woman hurried to catch up. She had the unnaturally smooth face of someone fending off the hands of time with wads of cash, the same expression on her face regardless of whether she'd just won a fortune or witnessed a lawnmower-based tragedy. The man approaching them extended his hand as he got closer.

"Reginald! So glad you could come! Meredith, you look delightful as usual! Are these the children? Hullo! I'm Rupert Smith Smyth-Jones, fourteenth Earl of Dormansland and this is my wife Pandora." A frenzy of handshakes and kissing of cheeks ensued.

"Rupert, it's my pleasure to present you Marcus and Zoe Rutherford, my nephew and niece from back home in New Zealand."

Rupert shook his hand while Pandora presented cheeks to be kissed. Zoe had to make do with a tussle of her hair, before they headed into a lounge area. Apparently Uncle Reggie just had to meet the Reverend. The lounge turned out to be the polar opposite to the hallway—light and airy with an expansive fireplace and comfortable couches under a chandelier. While the fireplace wasn't lit, the couches which faced each other looked very comfortable and the room promised great laughter and convivial conversation.

The Reverend turned out to be an earnest man who leaned forward at such an angle as to seem about to topple over. Marcus was surprised at how young he was, seeming to be in his early thirties. Most men of the cloth Marcus had known were in their late fifties at the youngest. The Reverend had a very ready smile which exposed an impressive set of teeth, and found everything 'superb', 'wonderful' and 'marvellous'. Marcus felt himself wilting under such a concentrated barrage of positivity. The Reverend got particularly excited when he learned that Uncle Reggie owned the estate to the south, and seemed keen to have a private chat about some of the parts of his very historic parish church that were in desperate need of maintenance. Mercifully they were called in to dinner before that could occur.

Dinner was a confusing affair, with many dishes and much cutlery. Aunty Meredith had warned them of this on the way over and Marcus and Zoe knew to start on the outside of the array of hardware and work their way in, and Uncle Reggie's advice to go slowly and keep an eye on what other people were doing stood them in good stead. Marcus reined in his natural inclination to start eating as soon as the food hit his plate. The Reverend blessed the food and their hosts and particularly the opportunity to meet new members of the parish. The conversations bouncing around the room evolved and flowed, sometimes one topic captivating the entire room, sometimes everyone just chatting with those sitting next to them.

Marcus liked their hosts. Pandora's assorted jewellery clinked together whenever she laughed, which was often, throwing her head back in abandon. The Earl made a point of including Marcus and Zoe in the conversations, asking them about their home and school life. Their daughter had just returned to University so the house was "eerily empty and quiet" according to Pandora. And it was good to have "young people around to breathe life back into the place". Marcus asked which University the daughter was attending which kicked off a lengthy discussion of the rollercoaster of emotions involved with applying to and getting into the correct university. After ten minutes he still didn't know where she was going to but could see that it had huge social significance wherever it was. Still, they were gracious hosts and he felt very fortunate to have been invited.

Another course was taken up by a lengthy answer to the question of how long the house had been in the family, what additions had been made and the gradual expansion or contraction of the estate's lands. It must be amazing to know your family tree so well and so far back, thought Marcus. It was easy for Marcus to think of their host as 'The Earl' and the other guest as 'The Reverend', ignoring their actual names and reducing them to their titles. He was just trying to figure out what that would make Pandora when dessert was served.

The meal had been presented by a staff of four who seemed to dance around the trails of conversation, never being caught between two people talking, and yet still delivering whichever course was being served, or collecting the dishes from the previous one. They were all young and attractive and impeccably dressed, white shirt or blouse and black trousers and with, rather weirdly, downcast eyes. During the whole evening, not one of them met Marcus's gaze. Marcus noticed his Uncle and Aunt made a point of saying 'thank you' each time, though the staff seemed to be wearing invisibility cloaks as far as their hosts were concerned.

Dessert turned out to be pavlova with whipped cream and strawberries. Pandora watched them nervously. "Is that right? We wanted something from New Zealand to make you welcome, and our cook assured us that pavlova was a New Zealand dish."

Uncle Reggie smiled evilly. "Don't let any Australians hear you say that," he told her.

"Don't listen to him, Pandora, it's perfect. Just like we would make at home," interjected Meredith. "As you can see," she continued, pointing to Zoe with her spoon.

Zoe looked up, the bowl half-finished, flakes of meringue sprinkled over the white tablecloth. "What?" she asked, having been concentrating on eating and therefore not having followed the conversation.

Eventually, the last of the meringue had been disposed of and the conversation began to be interspersed with subtle burps of appreciation as the meal drew to a close.

The Earl stood up, bowing his head towards Pandora. "Thank you for a lovely dinner my dear. Reginald!" Uncle Reggie flinched. "Will you join us in the drawing room for a snifter of brandy and a cigar?"

"Sure, I'd love to!" exclaimed Uncle Reggie, looking at Marcus. The Earl followed his gaze.

"Marcus, would you like to join us also?"

"Uh... sure!"

Surprised at being included, Marcus followed the group back into the drawing room, sitting beside Uncle Reggie on one of the couches. The Reverend sat opposite and the Earl busied himself at the drinks tray.

Uncle Reggie gave a wry grin when Marcus elected for ginger ale over the brandy that was on offer, stepping in to explain that Marcus had "overdone it" the night before when The Earl indicated that it would be alright for him to join them in a snifter. Marcus was secretly pleased that it was known he wasn't drinking because of a night of excess, feeling quite the hardened carouser while sipping his ginger ale. The Reverend joined Marcus and Uncle Reggie in turning down the offer of a cigar and, seeing he was alone in his desires, The Earl replaced them in the sideboard drawer with a wistful sigh.

As they settled into the deep leather couches, The Reverend gave Uncle Reggie a look over his glasses. "The parish priest invited me to give the sermon at St. Peter's last Sunday and I don't think I saw you there?"

Uncle Reggie shook his head.

"Or do you prefer St Mary's?"

"If you saw me in any of the churches I would recommend getting your eyes checked, Reverend. Or maybe it was a wedding, funeral or Christening. I must say you're making it difficult keeping my word to my wife."

The Reverend looked concerned. "Oh no, in what way?"

"She made me promise to avoid politics, religion and money, and straight off the bat you're giving me a hard time for not being one of your flock."

"Oh, we're not really talking about religion, are we? We're not disputing facets of dogma, now are we?"

Marcus piped up. "Why shouldn't you talk about politics, religion or money, Uncle?"

The Earl brought the last of the drinks over. "Because men get frightfully upset when strangers disagree with what they hold dear. Especially when it's not based on science. Matters of faith. Belief. That sort of thing."

Trying to justify his presence amongst the men-folk, Marcus continued with an insightful question. "But surely politics is at least a little scientific. My older brother was saying they have Political Science at university."

The Earl looked over condescendingly. "But if that was true we would only have one political party. The one with the policies driven by what science decides. Not much of a democracy then, surely!"

Uncle Reggie sipped his drink and asked quietly, "Are you saying that we have a democracy now?"

The question met with stillness. Marcus followed the confused glance that flitted between The Earl and The Reverend. He'd never seen Uncle Reggie anything but jovial. He hadn't moved, but all of a sudden Marcus was reminded of a snake waiting to strike, motionless until the prey had moved too close and could not escape.

"But of course! Britain has a great history of democracy! You've seen the elections."

Uncle Reggie considered his drink. "Sure, you have elections—first past the post so not representational. And leaving aside the monarch as a head of state, what about your upper house?"

The Reverend looked confused. "The House of Lords? My dear boy, whatever do you mean?"

"If democracy is the rule of the people by the people, surely you'd extend that to your upper house as well, no?"

"Oh no, the House of Lords reviews..."

"Marcus, the House of Lords—the 'Upper House'—reviews legislation and makes recommendations. Sounds pretty important right? Reverend how do you get a seat in the House of Lords?"

The Reverend smiled. "Well, the Prime Minister appoints them."

"Or...?"

The Reverend looked confused. "Or?"

"The House of Lords has more than the friends and family of the Prime Minister, right?"

Realisation dawned. "Oh, yes. There are 26 bishops in there too."

"And are they elected?"

"Oh yes, you see the Vacancy-in-See Committee first..."

"By the public?" interrupted Uncle Reggie.

"Oh, no, by the Church. But the bishops and the Lords all work very hard."

"Oh, I'm sure. How many are there sitting in the House of Lords now? Bishops and Lords?"

The Reverend was slower in answering. "I believe there are about 800."

"Wow, sounds like you'd need a big room to hold all those people."

"Actually the room can only sit about half of them."

Marcus saw that the atmosphere was getting a little toxic so tried to step in. "How did you come to have an unelected Upper House?"

Uncle Reggie smiled. "So originally the monarch was all powerful, right?

They made all the rules. And that's why there was so much intrigue and back-stabbing and wars, because being monarch meant you could make the rules which benefited your own family and friends and take money and lands from your enemies. And if the monarch ruled by the grace of God then if you managed to depose one it must have been God's will, right? Which therefore gave you as much right to rule as the previous ruler. Eventually the nobles and the church wanted to rein in the monarch and so they banded together and restricted the power of the crown—Magna Carter and all that. That was the Noblemen or the Lords reminding the crown of their power. And when that power evolved into parliament, the ability to make rules which benefited your family and friends transferred from the monarch to the ruling class. And that's where it's stuck. Other countries have had popular revolutions reminding the rulers that it's the people who have the power—France most notably, 'Vive la Revolution' and all that. But Britain has not, leading to a corrupt ruling class enriching each other and their friends, and choking public spending to keep the poor weak. The country that produced the National Health Service says that they can't afford to run it while giving uncontested billion pound contracts to their cronies. The institutions that are supposed to serve as a counterweight to that power—the free press and financial regulators—have been bought by those same cronies, so it's all a corrupt circle enriching all those on the inside." Uncle Reggie paused, holding up his finger and cocking his head as if listening for something.

"I say! That's rather a negative spin on things!"

"If you don't like it, why don't you go back..."

"And there it is!" Uncle Reggie shook a triumphant fist and grinned. "'If you don't like it go back to where you came from.' Please do let me know how long one has to live here before your opinions or criticisms are treated on their merits." His grin dropped and he leaned in, more serious now. "Your Aunt and I have chosen to live here! But I think that somewhere along the way the people in charge have forgotten that they represent the people. All the people, not just their rich friends. And at some point, somewhere along the line, the regular folk who can't feed themselves because you've cut their benefit or can't get their cancer drugs because you've strangled the public health system, they're going to say to themselves 'What do I have to lose?'"

The Reverend looked indignant. "You've given a very skewed and misleading representation of our country's politics!"

The Earl frowned. "The reason the contracts get given to people you know, is because you know you can trust them to deliver."

Uncle Reggie nodded. "That's true. It's important that they can deliver. But it does mean that the money stays in a closed circle, doesn't it? Nobody else gets a look in, even if they can deliver."

The Earl gave Uncle Reggie a long look. "One wonders if you would be so... civic minded if you were... invited into the inner circle?"

Uncle Reggie looked surprised. "Oh no!" he said. "I wouldn't join, but it has nothing to do with being noble or principled. I've got mine. If I was still some individual contributor doing a nine to five at a desk somewhere, of course I'd leap at the chance. And if I was greedy, I'd be looking at ways of making my million into ten million or my ten million into a hundred. But I have my trade which keeps me busy, I do a bit of travel and I have the love of my good wife, the company of family and friends. I don't go hungry and I give back to the community. I'm lucky."

In the silence that followed, Uncle Reggie leant back on the couch and turned slightly to Marcus. "Politics, religion and money," he stage-whispered. "It's all the same thing. Power."

The Earl tried valiantly to recover the evening, starting with the age-old English conversational topic of 'The Weather', before transitioning into 'Sport'. It seemed that there was a requirement to like a team or a physical pastime of some description. "I still don't know why you haven't taken up golf, Reginald! You've got the physique for it and it's a great way to stay fit. You're surrounded by the best golf courses in the world. What do you say? Shall I book us a tee time?"

Uncle Reggie demurred. "I have my swimming, I'm all set, thanks. Reverend, what do you do for exercise?"

The Reverend seemed taken aback. "Oh, I'm far too busy taking care of the pastoral needs of my parishes, the spiritual over the physical, you understand."

"Of course, of course," answered Uncle Reggie.

"And what about you, Marcus? Do you follow football? It's a pity the season has finished, it's a totally different experience watching the game in person."

Uncle Reggie quietly pointed out to Marcus that football meant soccer in the UK, rather than rugby back home in New Zealand.

"Ah, no, we get coverage back home, but I don't have a favourite team at all. I'm not really into sports too much."

Uncle Reggie stepped in. "I think Marcus is more cerebral, like yourself, Reverend."

That seemed to be an uncontroversial thing to say, and provoked much nodding and semi formed grunts of agreement. The tone of the evening seemed to be recovering from Uncle Reggie's earlier rant.

INGENUE

The evening had wound down quickly and they'd left the Earl's manor house with waves and promises of coffee and cake one afternoon later in the week. The weather had behaved and followed the forecast of a dry night, the near full moon light illuminating their trek back to the house.

The walk back home was highlighted by Aunt Meredith interrogating Uncle Reggie on whether he had been well-behaved over the cigars and brandy. Despite his protestations of innocence, or perhaps because of them, Meredith turned to Marcus. "Was he well-behaved?" she asked with one eyebrow cocked.

Put on the spot like that, Marcus could not pretend to be focussing on walking along the path, and had to come up with something. "Um, it was all very civilised, I thought," he managed.

Aunt Meredith hmmed while giving him the side eye. "I'll get the real story from Pandora, I think."

"What did you and Zoe and Pandora talk about?" asked Marcus to shift the focus away from contentious conversations. He was surprised when Meredith seemed to colour slightly in the moonlight and changed the subject. He made a mental note to check with Zoe later. Two could play that game!

The next morning Marcus breakfasted with the others. The bustle of the kitchen reminded him of the chaos of his house back home—big families somehow generating a singular collective noise just by everyone doing their own thing. Zoe was set to go horse riding again, this time apparently through the forests along the paths that Marcus had explored. He suddenly realised that he was not going to be required to look after Zoe very much at all. He was so used to having to look after her and he had quite resigned himself to spending much of the holiday on custodial duties and now that he wasn't tied to keeping her entertained he started to think about what else he might like to spend his time doing.

If he'd been the athletic type he might have made his way north to the paintball or laser tag arenas. Obviously, an equestrian would have tagged along with Zoe. If he'd been the gregarious type he might have tried to connect with the folks he'd met at the pub. A lothario might have attempted to chat up Samantha or Marie or find a girlfriend for the summer. If he'd been an Indiana Jones type he might have headed back into London or explored locally. But truth be told, when he wasn't looking after his sister he could normally be found on the computer playing one or other video game with his older brother. But his PC was a million miles away and the only other thing he was really into was reading. And so on day five of their holiday, Marcus found himself heading to the library to see what books his Uncle had either inherited with the house or collected in his travels. Nothing wrong with curling up with a good book.

Just before he entered the Library, Marcus paused. Instead of entering the room, he peered inside, taking in the position of the bookshelves on opposing walls, and where the fireplace was situated. Then he stood at the door to the neighbouring Garden Room, marking in his mind what was against the shared wall, before repeating the process at the door of the Dining Room which was to the right of the Library. Finally he actually entered the Library and stood in front of the closest bookshelf.

A voice holding barely suppressing a chuckle followed him into the room.

"Were you... checking you were in the right room? Or did you forget something?"

He turned to see the patient wrapped in bandages standing at the door. Her large sunglasses were tucked precariously into a fold of the wrappings. Now that he was seeing her in more light, even though she was still wearing her dressing gown, he could tell that she was slim—bordering on thin and with a disproportionately large chest. His ears finally caught up with his eyes and he blushed.

"Truth?" he managed, smiling at his own embarrassment.

She nodded.

"I was just checking if the library had a secret door. If any of the bookshelves might have opened into one of the other rooms."

Her voice had dimples. "And?"

"It doesn't look likely. I'm Marcus."

"Shon - Ingenue." She corrected herself.

"'On-zhen-oo'," Marcus tried. "Is that an Irish name? Chinese?" he asked, frowning.

"It's spelled I-n-g-e-n-u-e. It's French."

Marcus tried it, using an excessive French accent. He wasn't sure if she approved.

"I was born Shona Jones, but my team came up with Ingenue as a professional name. Like Madonna, or Cher. Are you enjoying England so far?"

"Yes," replied Marcus.

"How cute!" Ingenue exclaimed, "'Yiss', you've got an adorable accent."

"My accent?" asked Marcus. "Do I have an accent?".

"You do have a very slight 'excent'," said Ingenue.

Marcus couldn't tell if the teasing was good-natured or not, so elected to try and change the subject. "How long are you going to be all wrapped up?"

"Might be a few more days. I'm going crazy bored though. I'm allowed back on the treadmill now so at least I get some exercise."

"What did you do before then?"

"I played my uke, read a few scripts my team sent through, binged a couple of series on TV. That sort of thing."

"It's a pity it's not Halloween, you could lurch out of bushes and scare the neighbourhood kids."

She started to laugh and then stopped with a sharp intake of breath. "Ooh that smarts," she said, holding her side.

"I was going to find a book to read. Have you read any of these?" he asked, indicating the shelves.

"Ah... with the eye surgery I can't really be exposed to much bright light and without the light I can't really read, so..."

"Fair enough," Marcus continued. "Hey - Francine makes a mean cookie, I could see if she has any left?"

"Francine is the housekeeper? Ah... I'm on a 1500 calorie per day diet, so I don't think I can fit that in. But thanks. Hmmm... cookies. Haven't had one of those for a while."

"OK, well I'm going to find a book and read it if you wanted to hang out?"

"Sure, that sounds ok." She left, coming back with her ukulele and metal bottle of water and set herself down slightly askew on the couch facing the fireplace with her back angled towards the window. Marcus still hadn't finished looking at the books on the first bookshelf. It seemed as if someone had just bought a complete collection of classics—Robert Louis Stevenson, Conan Arthur Doyle, a smattering of Brontës and Austens... shelf after shelf of culture in bulk. Marcus was vaguely aware that a lot of the books were probably set or written in the general geographical area, but he wasn't in the mood for ye olde adventures or costumed dramas.

The next shelf was a bit more modern. Twentieth Century, anyway. Ingenue came over to see what was on offer and as Marcus' hand lingered on The Diary of Anne Frank she peered at the cover. "Hey did you hear the controversy about that one: her dad removed all the sex bits. I guess that's what you get when your parents edit you, huh?" Marcus smiled and nodded.

His hand trailed over the covers as he read the titles, considered them and then moved on. Too much choice maybe. He watched Ingenue out of the corner of his eye and paused when he came to Nabakov's Lolita, trying to see if there was any response. She might not have been watching because there was nothing, so he continued on. They'd read The Catcher in the Rye and The Lord of the Flies in English at school, and The Lord of the Rings had been demolished after having seen the movies, but nothing else really appealed. The bottom few shelves were taken up with board games, Monopoly resting slightly askew on top of Jenga and Guess Who?

The third bookshelf held more contemporary titles, and the cover art was much more racy than those on the other shelves. Marcus guessed that these were the books that previous guests had discarded or swapped after they'd read them: books whose goal was to match the brain to the now relaxed and stress-free bodies. Marcus didn't really have an opinion of the books but recognised some of them as ones his mother had churned through and therefore considered them suspect.

He looked over to the last bookcase. Ingenue had returned to her couch and was looking at her phone. This one seemed to have mainly non-fiction books, the bottom two shelves filled with 32 thick brown bound Encyclopaedia Britannica volumes. Above these were a few dictionaries, a thesaurus and a chaotic collection of various knitting magazines all lying down to fit into the mis-sized shelf, their spines facing upwards.

On one of the top shelves, almost forgotten amongst a row of hard-backed celebrity cooking books, was a narrow volume entitled The History of Felstead. Marcus fetched it down and opened it. It was signed by the author and looked to be a self-published effort with dubious binding. Upon closer inspection the signature turned out to be above an inscription To Reg, This is what you're getting yourself into.

"As good as any," thought Marcus, heading to the couch. The couch was wide enough that he wasn't crowding Ingenue and he settled in to give the book his full attention.

The tome was actually a collection of snippets from other books which mentioned Felstead, so it opened with medieval references, the pages splattered with curly f's and s's and trailing e's. Tax yields in shillings, legal rulings and fines with the blocks of text almost incomprehensible with strange occupations and syntax suggesting hidden layers of meaning and shorthand. It was a view of the lives of the local populace which could have been repeated at any time during the ages, the actors described by their craft, the notable events being crimes large or small. One in particular caught Marcus' eye: the disposal of a horse after its owner had been executed for pickpocketing. No mention of the victim's name, but the name of the pickpocketer rang a bell. Tobias Goodacre—exactly the same name as the poacher who had been at the pub! Marcus briefly considered whether the same man had been bouncing around the countryside for the past few centuries before deciding that the poacher and the pickpocket were probably closely related but distinct human beings.

"What did you find?" asked Ingenue, looking over at him.

Marcus told her about the poachers at the Duck's Bark and then about the same name appearing in the history.

"So, do you think that the whole family is a family of thieves?" asked Ingenue.

"I don't know, that's only two people over all those years, so maybe not. But I'll bet it's hard to get out of the cycle once you're in it. I guess that's why some families get a bad reputation."

Marcus continued reading, his thoughts drifting off from the page into a world where nothing seemed to really change. The same families farmed, fell in love, married, gave birth, got ill, died, season after season and year after year. Lived at the mercy of the weather, a crop surplus one year, a drought the next. The noteworthy events with the notable actors ignored the struggles of the regular folk: two sentences summed up a local landowner backing a rebellion, being executed and their lands reclaimed by the crown and given to a new noble. Marcus imagined the farmer toiling behind his oxen, one day paying his taxes to one lord, the next to someone new. And greeting the news with a shrug: the view from behind the oxen wouldn't change.

Francine interrupted his reverie, asking Ingenue if she'd like her snack in the library. Ingenue asked what it was today, Francine answering "raw carrot sticks and celery". Ingenue said she'd have them there on the couch if she could. "Of course you can, my dear. What about you, Marcus? I think I have a couple of those cookies left. Or maybe a slice of my ginger loaf with butter?"

Marcus smiled at Ingenue before answering, "Could I get some carrot and celery too? If there's enough of course?"

Francine looked from Marcus to Ingenue and laughed. "Of course! Won't be a jiffy!" And then she bustled off. She returned not long after with a pair of plates, each piled with fingers of vegetables. "I'm two doors down, so if you feel like anything else just sing out." She left them with a jug of water with a couple of slices of lemon floating around inside and a pair of glasses.

After they'd finished the snack, Ingenue asked if he would mind if she played her ukulele. He said no, thinking himself well-prepared after a lifetime of having to tune out Zoe's prattling while playing first person shooters on the internet. He listened for a minute or two before diving back into the book. "You're pretty good," he told her, able to recognise the song she was playing. She didn't say anything, but inclined her head slightly in acknowledgement.

The book talked about something called "beating the bounds". Apparently once a year the whole village would walk a path through the parish, learning the edges of the property plots. And to help the knowledge stick, the elders would make the lessons physical—throwing children into gorse bushes, making them jump over water-filled ditches, or pulling them through a hedge, the minor physical pain apparently more permanently embedding the lesson. And the communal event would have brought the parish together, thought Marcus.

Marcus put down his book and focused on Ingenue's playing. "We're a roaring fire away from how they lived in the old days," he observed, indicating the fireplace opposite them. Ingenue may have smiled in response, or she may have grimaced, Marcus didn't know. The lack of facial features was beginning to get in the way of any real communication.

Back to the book. Eventually, the content petered out into descriptions of the ownerships of various limited liability companies and finally spluttered to a halt in the early 1900s. Marcus hadn't enjoyed the ending of the book nearly as much as the beginning but found that his interest was piqued. Maybe there would be other books with more information about the neighbouring area. He got up and returned the book to the shelf where it had come from. But there were no other books there with similar titles. The clock above the fireplace was showing noon and Francine came back inquiring if Ingenue would be joining them for lunch or if she would prefer to dine in one of the other rooms.

"Would you mind if I had my lunch in here? It might be a little light for my eyes in the kitchen."

"No problem at all, I'll bring it through now," Francine said, already heading to the kitchen.

"Thanks," Ingenue called after her. She turned back to Marcus. "I'm supposed to hit the treadmill after lunch, but we can catch up after that if you want to?"

"Sure, that sounds fun," replied Marcus, already getting to his feet to see what Francine had whipped up this time.

It turned out to be a healthy salad served with slabs of turkey and a loganberry sauce. She'd rustled up some homemade ginger beer, mentioning that making the cloudy concoction was a hobby of William's and that this batch was the first one that hadn't exploded while fermenting. She was convinced William was also making an alcoholic version.

Lunch was a convivial affair, with Uncle Reggie and Aunty Meredith joining them in good spirits. Apparently, some deal or another was getting close to closing and they were very happy with how things were going.

"So what did you get up today, Marcus?" Aunty Meredith asked.

"I found a fascinating book in the library—The History of Felstead."

"Oh yes," interjected Uncle Reggie, "Samuel Barrow is a lovely guy. He's the local historian. He was very welcoming when we arrived and told us many tales about the local area. I think he autographed the book didn't he?"

"Absolutely. Did he just write the one book? It's fascinating!"

"I think so. That was more of a collection. He did give Aunty Meredith a book for her birthday the Friday before you two arrived, but that was written by someone else. The estate is briefly mentioned, so I guess that matches what you're after? Where's the book that Sam gave you, dear?"

"I think it's in the den. Let me check." Minutes later she came back with a brand new paperback in large format.

Marcus smiled back his thanks and finished his lunch, before heading back to the library and curling up on the couch.

Sure enough, the first page of the book was in the same handwriting as the Felstead History's dedication. The subject of the book was corruption and the flow of ill-gotten wealth and how the UK was an international clearinghouse for the legitimisation of those funds. Marcus reflected on the tone of Uncle Reggie's rant at dinner the previous night and wondered if Aunt Meredith had been given the book because of Uncle Reggie's point of view. Or whether the book was evidence supporting the rant. Or if both Uncle Reggie and the book were wrong, maybe the rant and the book were just two expressions of the same shared delusion. He flipped to the footnotes of the book. They seemed impressive—interviews, pointers to respectable newspapers and magazines. Shrugging, he hit the index and found the references to the family who had sold Uncle Reggie the estate. Regardless of whether Uncle Reggie was right or not, it would be interesting to find out more about the purchase. It might even give more credence to Uncle Reggie's explanation of how he came into his wealth. Which would satisfy the interest around dinner tables back home.

Settling into the couch again, Marcus dived into the book, starting with the indexed references before reading more widely, trying to go upstream from the references to contextualise what he found there.

Lost in his readings, he didn't notice that Ingenue had returned until she plonked herself down on the couch. She was breathing heavily but seemed to be wearing the same bathrobe as before.

"What are you reading?" she asked.

"A book which mentions the previous owners of the estate," he answered. "Turns out they were allegedly involved with moving money for one or other of the Russian republics. The author likes that word, allegedly. Does it mean that he can't be sued? Anyway, they were an extended family who bought the estate with money that they were funnelling from mines and oil interests in Central Asia. Apparently, they needed a cash injection for fines, bribes and legal fees from one or other of their escapades with other billionaire oligarchs. They were worried about being kidnapped—their former partners weren't beyond hiring a bunch of mercenaries and sending them to 'aid in the arrest' of their rivals. Great when you're onside with them but if you have a disagreement... Here's a photo of them."

"Wow, they're short! Look, there's a taxi in the background. That must make the father only a little taller than five feet six. Does it mention anything more about the estate?"

"Just that they made a big loss on the sale due to needing the money in a hurry. Uncle Reggie happened to be in the right place at the right time."

"Lucky!"

"How was the treadmill?"

"Dire. I've lost so much fitness since the operations that it feels like I'm starting from scratch all over again. I'm just lucky that my trainer has me on a gentle schedule until the stitches come out."

They chatted about this and that, the periodic pauses feeling more comfortable than awkward.

"Where did you go last night?"

"Oh, we went to the Earl's mansion for dinner. Lucky we went last night as they say we're getting a storm tonight. Full moon, too. Awwwoooooo!" He was about to go and find Francine—to check what time dinner was—when a commotion from the kitchen attracted his attention. He leapt to his feet to check it out, arriving at the kitchen to see that the bifold doors looking out over the lawn to the north were pulled open and everybody was spilled out onto the lawn looking at the sky. As he got closer he could understand why. There was a strong smell of smoke in the air and in the distance to the north a flickering red glow reflected off the underside of the clouds.

FIRE IN THE NIGHT

"C'mon kids, let's go and see if we can help. We've got the swimming pools if the fire department needs more water." Uncle Reggie shrugged his windbreaker on and headed out the door. Behind him, Aunt Meredith had a phone in her hand and was dialling.

"I'll make sure the fire department knows about it. I'll wait here," she said.

Uncle Reggie headed out along the path on the other side of the lake, setting a brisk pace. Zoe skipped along beside him, the aches and pains from the day's horse riding forgotten. They travelled on the same paths that they had taken to the Earl's the previous night, reaching the hill with the commanding view over the surrounding lands in very good time - a good two hours of daylight remaining, though the low-slung, heavy rain clouds were painting the available light a murky purple hue.

Uncle Reggie paused there, peering towards the Earl's mansion.

"Oh, good, it looks like the fire department is there."

Marcus couldn't see any fire trucks. There was a collection of cars chaotically parked in front of the mansion, the lights of the fire flashing on their paintwork and shadowy silhouetted figures flitting between them.

The mansion was well alight, the strengthening wind providing occasional respite from the smell, showers of embers rising in columns of orange. It was a surreal view from the hilltop.

The silhouettes darting between the cars seemed to have stopped to perform some sort of ceremony.

Uncle Reggie radiated concern. "What the - "

The unmistakable sound of a gun going off rebounded over the countryside.

A moment later the dark shadowy figures, still backlit by the fire, seemed to look straight at the three of them on the hill. Zoe shrank from the malevolent gaze. At that instant, some of the shadows started across the field towards them. Dark figures picked out against the lighter green of the fields. Headlights flicked on among the cars at the mansion and the squeal of tyres joined the crackle of the fire.

"Time to go," Uncle Reggie decided, leading the way back down the hill, Marcus and Zoe following closely behind. Terror gave their legs wings and they reached the lane separating the left from the right sides of the estate in about half the time it had taken them to get there. Marcus reached for the gate that would take them back to the House, but Uncle Reggie stopped him. The lane was crooked and lined with trees, hiding them from the pursuing shadows.

"Marcus, wait. Listen. There's a bunker in the pasture in front of our cottage, you know where the cottage is, right? Take Zoe there until it's safe to come out. The door is hidden, but line up the lights from the fish farm and the power lines and where those lights are on top of each other you'll find a door in the ground. There's enough food in there for a hundred people for a hundred days. The code is Aunt Meredith's birthday. Go quickly! Look after your sister!"

And before Marcus could stop him, Uncle Reggie was off, loping in huge strides across the farmland. In the silence that followed, Zoe looked up at him, questioning.

"This way!" he told her, taking her hand in his and heading along the path that headed up to the forested side of the left-hand loop of the estate. Zoe was trying to keep up, but was having trouble: whether it was a length-of-stride thing or all the time she'd spent on the horses, Marcus didn't know. He slowed down enough so she wasn't a dead weight at the end of his arm and they concentrated on where they were putting their feet. Marcus heard something off to their right and stopped dead, holding up his hand.

"What is it?" Zoe whined.

"Shhh!" he hissed. The sound of their heavy breathing was smothered by the wind in the trees, but beyond the lines of trees on the country lane where they'd just left Uncle Reggie, they could hear shouting and running, and then through the leaves the lights of a car. Car doors slammed. They backed away from the noise, continuing on their way back up the hill through the forest.

The wind was stronger now and carried the odd drop of rain. Marcus was glad Zoe wasn't asking questions so they could focus on their escape in silence. They reached the part of the hill with the electricity pylon and Marcus remembered the potted ground. He slowed down and warned Zoe about the way ahead, bringing his mouth close to her ear to keep the noise down. His initial attempts were blown away on the wind so he spoke normally, trusting that the weather would keep their presence hidden. They picked their way carefully up the hill in the shadow of the powerlines, Marcus noting that each of the pylons had red lights at the top, red and blinking. He hoped that it would be easy to find the door to the bunker. He didn't want to think about anything beyond that.

They reached the top of the hill and followed the driveway around past the fishery to the lane which led to the cottage. Again they got wafts of smoke on the wind. The rain, big thick drops, was still only hesitantly falling but the sky boiled with colour. In the west, the sun was beginning to set, above them the purple-black clouds still reflected the fire of the Earl's estate and in the distance they could see other columns of embers dotted around the countryside.

Marcus was relieved when they were swallowed by the tree-lined lane to the cottage—the evidence of such widespread violence truly terrified him.

He silenced the voice in his head which kept asking what was happening and why, and concentrated on his surroundings. The only thing that mattered was finding the bunker and getting Zoe inside. To get to safety.

They got to the cottage without incident and Marcus took them directly into the pasture in front of it. He'd gone maybe twenty paces into the waist-high grass before turning around. First, he found the blinking light on top of the pylon and followed it down to where the lights on top of the fishery containers should be, but they were blocked by the trees. He headed deeper into the pasture, followed by a bewildered Zoe. He traced a bizarre path across the field, lurching for ten or twenty paces, turning around to peer through the darkness at the lights, trying to guess which trees would block the lights and which direction he'd need to take to get a clear view. Then lurching forward again.

Zoe held her tongue, seeing the look of concentration on her brother's face and knowing something important was going on but not sure what it was or how she fitted into it. The rain was now torrential. Marcus, constantly blowing the rain away from his nose, made another lurch across the grassland.

It wasn't so much that there was no light, rather that there were three white lights on top of the containers, and such was the closeness of the containers to the pylon, that the places where the lights aligned were far away from each other. He'd reached the first intersection of lights and spent ten minutes kicking around and looking at the ground with no luck before heading off to the next one. Another ten minutes crisscrossing the field before the lights lined up and another fruitless search. He was heading to the last intersection when Zoe started to cry.

"I'm cold and wet, Marcus. What are we doing out here? Where is Uncle Reggie? Why don't we go back to the house?"

Realising that she wouldn't go on without some sort of explanation, he took a second to compose himself. "Uncle Reggie wants us to find a door in the ground to a bunker. It's really important that we find it, otherwise he wouldn't have sent us out in the rain."

She sniffled and wiped her nose on her arm. "A metal door in the ground?"

Shocked, he nodded.

"It's over there. Can we go home now?"

"Show me!"

She led him back the way they'd come. "It's where the middle light and the pylon light line up," she said patiently, pointing to an area adjacent to one of the paths they'd bulldozed through the grass. Sure enough, lurking in the shadowy undergrowth was a door, hidden—unless you were almost on top of it—by the surrounding weeds and wildflowers.

Marcus smiled at her and examined the door. It was the same size as a house door, and although at first glance had looked like a sheet of rusting metal, it turned out to have some sort of plastic or rubber coating, coloured to look like rust and textured to look old and decayed. Marcus pulled on the handle, half expecting it to come away in his hand, so convincing was the decrepit camouflage. Instead, it lifted easily, revealing a stairway. Low lights flickered on, pointing down from the walls just above the steps to light their way. As they descended, Marcus noticed that none of the light escaped the stairwell. The stairs stopped about ten feet down at a plain white metal door with a shiny metal lever serving as a door handle, set in a white metal wall. Marcus couldn't see any digital keypad or anything to put Aunty Meredith's birthdate into, and the door had no lock. He breathed out in relief when the lever succumbed to his attempts to open it, the door opening with an ease belying its weight. He turned to Zoe and told her to close the door at the top of the stairs before taking in the sight of the bunker.

THE HOLE

It was cramped. And white. Right by the door was what looked like a black metal vacuum cleaner with some sort of thick metal chimney disappearing into the ceiling. Three bunk beds squished against the wall, one on top of the other, with brand new bare mattresses without sheets or pillows, the bottom bunk at floor level. Opposite the beds, crammed along the wall on the other side, were a floor-to-ceiling set of shallow shelves (empty), with a 17-inch LCD screen on the top shelf. Beside them was a mini kitchenette, with a half-sized sink with tap and a double gas hob. The bunks took up half the length of the bunker. The remaining space on the left was split between an open cupboard and the bathroom, a toilet on one side and a shower on the other. There was some form of fuse box in the cupboard about halfway up the wall and a large cardboard box almost filling the bottom half.

It looked brand new. It looked empty. It certainly didn't look like it could hold a hundred people for a hundred days. Maybe there was something in the cardboard box. Closer inspection revealed that while everything else in the room was new, the box looked a little more worn, scuffed and torn at the corners. It had apparently contained a bulk load of toilet paper and Marcus desperately hoped that they'd find something more edible than bog roll. Flipping open the flaps on the box, Marcus peered inside. And felt tears well up. Nothing. Nothing! The bottom of the box stared back at him.

With a growl, his stomach let him know that afternoon tea had been a long while ago, and that he was quite ready for a meal thank you very much.

The adrenaline which had powered their headlong rush away from the Earl's mansion and then through the forest and pasture to the bunker seeped away, leaving him feeling drained and distraught. He staggered the three steps to the bunks where Zoe sat watching him and collapsed on the middle bed beside her. She started to cry quietly and he held her close so that she couldn't see his tears. She fell asleep soon after and so he got up, turned off the light and joined her on the bunk.

He awoke from a dream where he was wandering through a forest at night. Through the canopy, he could see the full moon, and the moonbeams occasionally pierced through the leaves to light his path. In the distance he could hear the crack of something large walking through the forest, breaking twigs and rustling through the bushes. As he turned in that direction, he could smell smoke and the trees ahead started to erupt into flames. He started running away from the flames but the forest grew denser and the flames drew closer. The trees were exploding into flames, the explosions showering him with sparks and his pace slowed because of the undergrowth. As panic grew his breath became ragged. He reached a wall of unburnt trees, the gaps between them filled in with creepers, bushes and a head-high hedge. He threw himself at it, struggling and thrashing until, finally, he burst into a clearing, bathed in the full moonlight. Uncle Reggie came towards him, with something urgent he needed to tell him. Just before he could speak, Marcus woke up.

He looked around. The light was back on, and the austere surroundings glared back at him. The bathroom door was closed, suggesting Zoe's whereabouts. Marcus went over to the interior of the entrance door. There was a shiny metal bar on this side as well, but there were three marks painted on the door along the arc that the end of the metal bar travelled. The first was marked with an O, the current (middle) spot with a C and lastly an L. With a bit of experimentation, Marcus worked out that the three heavy locking rods hidden within the thick door were engaged when the bar was in the L for "locked" setting. It didn't take an Einstein to work out that the O meant "open" and the C "closed", and Marcus was grateful that nobody had discovered them during the night when they had merely closed the door.

Zoe came over to see what he was doing and he showed her the locking system and explained how the rod had to point to the L for them to be safe inside. They looked for food but found nothing more than what they'd seen the previous night. The black vacuum cleaner beside the bunks with the pipe disappearing into the ceiling turned out to be some sort of air filtration system. The cupboards under the sink and hob were empty and the monitor on the top shelf was unplugged and unconnected. There were power points spotted around the walls, but it looked like someone had just installed the bunker and then left before even attempting to make it liveable. At least there was water and light. And it wasn't cold underground. But Marcus could feel himself getting angry. He'd been able to focus on getting to the bunker and ignoring all the unpleasantness of last night only because he'd believed Uncle Reggie when he'd said that the bunker would be all they needed. Food for one hundred people for a hundred days! Pah! There was nothing here!

"Fuck Uncle Reggie! He's so full of shit. What are we going to eat? There's no food here."

Zoe looked up at him from the bunk. "We could order pizza?" she asked, holding up the ugly phone Uncle Reggie had given them.

Marcus' anger disappeared. Of course! They could ring Uncle Reggie, find out where he was, maybe ring William and get picked up, before they knew it they would be having one of Francine's full English breakfasts and going for a swim in the pool. Marcus had left his phone in his jacket back at the house, left behind in the rush to get to the Earl's to see if they could help. He shared a smile with Zoe as he took the phone from her.

"We won't be able to order pizza or any delivery food. We're hiding, so nobody can know that we're here. But we can see what's going on." He went through the Contacts list, dialling each number. Uncle Reggie's and Aunt Meredith's phones had an out of service message on them. Francine's and William's came back with messages saying that the voicemail boxes were full. The house phones at the cottage and the house both just rang and rang. Zoe saw the hope drain from Marcus's face as number after number came up blank.

"What about Mum? Or Granny? Or Dad?" Zoe asked.

Marcus tried the house phone at Granny's. "Your account cannot make international calls. Please visit one of our stores to upgrade your account. Or visit us online at..."

Marcus tried the police. Then when the call wouldn't go through he remembered the emergency numbers were different in the UK. But even when he tried 999, the call didn't go through. Just in case, he tried 911. Nothing.

Zoe read his disappointment. "No pizza?"

Marcus handed back the phone. "No pizza."

Marcus racked his brain. He figured they were safe enough if they stayed put, but they would eventually starve. The cottage was just beside the pasture, so maybe he could sneak over there and raid the cupboards. Besides, the crowd that they'd seen at the Earl's surely would have moved on by now?

He glanced at the time on the phone. 10 am. Afternoon tea the previous day had been at 3 pm. 19 hours without food. He made a decision.

"I'm going to try the cottage for food," he told Zoe. "Keep the door closed and only open it if you hear me do this knock." He rapped off four knocks, paused and then two more. "Let's just check that you can hear the knocks through the door." The last thing he wanted was to be stuck outside. It turned out that the door had great insulation, but Zoe could still make out the pattern. "Stay near the door. I shouldn't be long. The cottage is just over there."

He heard the lock engage behind him and then headed gingerly up the stairs. As soon as he stepped out, the lights on the stairs flickered on. He carefully went up the stairs, planting his feet on the second step from the top which almost caused his body to be bent in half with his ear close to the door. Nothing. Taking a deep breath, he pushed against the door. He'd been used to the heavy door behind him, forgetting how easily this door opened the previous night, so put a bit too much effort into opening it and realised too late as it flung open.

Bright sunlight streamed into the staircase, temporarily blinding him. The musical tweeting of birdlife filled his ears and the sweet smell of wildflowers filled his nostrils. He remained frozen in place, ears probing the sounds, trying to hear any alarm or indication that he'd been seen. Nothing.

He crept out, keeping low to the ground, below the level of the hip-high grass. Looking like a meerkat peering at his environs, Marcus scanned his horizon. The pasture was surrounded by trees on all sides, with a gate in the southeastern corner that led to the cottage. The light on top of the pylon blinked red, but the lights on the shipping containers were off. He tried to estimate the distance to each edge of the pasture, attempting to gain some sort of navigation aid that might help him on his return. Eventually, he figured it out. It was a three-step process but he was confident that he'd be able to find the door even in the dark. It involved drawing a mental line from the middle of one side of the pasture to the edge of the other, then cross-referencing that with a line a quarter along the long side of the pasture.

He gently closed the door, noticing how hard it was to see, even from so close. He also saw that the previous night's rain-soaked trek through the grasslands had beaten down a track of sorts through the pasture, passing ten feet from the door. Luckily the weight of him and Zoe going over the path twice had made it more solid, and the last ten feet to the door they'd gone single file and as a result the path didn't go right up to the door, just nearby. Marcus realised that he'd be able to follow the path back to the bunker on his return instead of constantly looking at the treeline trying to navigate. Unfortunately, there was nothing noticeable about the part of the path where he'd need to leave it to cover the last ten feet, but his mental navigation steps should suffice.

Keeping slightly bent over, he made his way carefully back the way they'd come during the night. He couldn't really believe what they'd seen the previous night and spent some time trying to come up with a scenario that could explain the gunshot, the chase, the fires. He came to the gate separating the pasture from the lane leading to the cottage. On the other side stood the still-smouldering husk of the cottage. The glass conservatory a shattered ruin. The roof had gone entirely and fragments of the scorched walls were the only things remaining, though the interior was heaped with charred rubble and ash.

Marcus gazed at the carnage for a moment without comprehending what he was seeing. The smell of the fire wafted towards him, and the moment it hit his nose, the situation all of a sudden became real. Despite all evidence to the contrary, Marcus thought that there might be some food remaining and was readying himself to climb over the gate when he heard a yell, a bang and a high pitched whine ripping the air beside his ear. He fled in terror, sprinting back down the path. Another shot rang out, echoing across the pasture and giving Marcus an extra burst of speed.

He felt that he was somewhere near the door and leapt into the long grass beside the path towards where he thought it might be. He had guessed well and landed beside the door. He wasted no time and opened it, throwing himself inside before closing it awkwardly and almost stumbling down the steps, coming to a crash at the door. In his eagerness, he rapped more times than he should before pausing and doing the last two knocks more clearly. The door swung open revealing Zoe's small face. He darted inside, swinging the door closed swiftly, slamming it closed and locking it securely.

He took some deep ragged breaths and tried to compose himself. Zoe looked up at him expectantly and waited. "That... didn't go as well as I thought it would," he managed. "I think it might be better if we waited."

"I'm hungry," Zoe reminded him.

"Well you might have to wait a little bit longer," Marcus continued, the memory of the noise the bullet had made as it whizzed past him still very vivid. "Tell you what, I'll go down to the house after dark. You saw how much food they had there, right? I should be able to find something to eat. And there's the greenhouse and the fishery and the lake as well. Can you wait until tonight? It's a long time, but can you be brave?"

Zoe put her "brave girl" face on and nodded solemnly.

"That means no complaining or being grumpy though." She nodded again.

He hugged her. "We'll be ok, we just need to be patient," he told her. "We've got enough water, right? And what did Poppy used to tell us when we were hungry?"

She smiled and yelled, "Have a drink of water!" She was silent for a while, thinking. "I miss Poppy," she said finally. Their maternal grandfather had died two years earlier, as good a topic as any to distract his sister from her hunger, so Marcus reminded her of things she used to say and do and then Zoe reminded him of things he'd forgotten. The day turned into a freewheeling "do you remember when" session. Whenever the topic came too close to the events of the holiday, Marcus steered them back to friends and family back home. In this way, plus copious cupped handfuls of water and visits to the toilet, the morning slowly gave way to afternoon.

Marcus decided that he would need a nap in the afternoon if he was to be out at night. He grabbed the top bunk and Zoe took the middle one. As soon as he closed his eyes to try and sleep he realised he was terrified. Someone had tried to shoot him. Someone had burned the cottage. Someone had burned the Earl's mansion and shot someone—probably the Earl. Or Pandora. Or both. And now, in a few hours, he would be putting himself in harm's way. On purpose. He couldn't see any other way around it though: they needed food. They couldn't order delivery. The police weren't answering.

All the problems with his plan flitted through his mind. He knew that the fishery containers were locked up pretty tight, so getting in and helping himself to one of the fish was probably not going to work. The fishing lake required a fishing line. The garden would only give them raw vegetables. Even if the mansion was intact, they would still have to cook the food. And there was no gas bottle for the hob. Even if there was one, Marcus didn't know how to hook it up. They had electric appliances back home. And all that presupposed he could get there at night without getting shot.

Eventually, he dropped off, waking up from a dreamless sleep. He carefully looked over the edge of the bunk to see what Zoe was doing. She lay on her bunk, staring at the wall. Her mouth moved but no sound came out.

"What are you doing, Zoe?" he asked.

She smiled. "I'm counting my heartbeats," she told him. At least she wasn't worrying about their situation. Or their hunger. They spoke of this and that until it was time to go, Marcus deeming that 1 am was probably late enough to avoid anyone. He took a deep breath and kissed Zoe on the top of her head. "No falling asleep instead of letting me in, right?"

She smiled back at him, trusting. He smiled too, then carefully and slowly slid the door open and peered around the edge. The lights on the steps flicked on, revealing an empty stairwell. Marcus focused on his breathing to slow his heartbeat, moving slowly up the stairs. Before he reached the top he turned and signalled for Zoe to close the door and go inside. The door outside sprang eagerly open and he paused, once again alert to any danger, but hearing nothing except the night. He left the staircase and closed the door after himself. The lights aligned perfectly, and he tried his navigation shortcut to see how it held up in the night. Surprisingly well, he thought. Again he crouch-walked back along the path he and Zoe had worn into the grass, not sure if he should be thankful or cursing the full moon overhead, or the lack of cloud cover. The moonlight illuminated his way and he moved on shaking legs back towards the gate to the cottage.

He crouched down beside the gate, listening intently. Nothing. He gingerly put his hand on the gate, cringing at the slight creak from the hinges. There was no repeat of that morning's events, so he slowly climbed the gate and jogged down the lane which led to the fishing containers. Through the hedge on his right, he could make out the complex of shipping containers, noting that there was a car parked in the middle of them. "Maybe a guard?" he thought to himself as he continued along the lane past the cattlestop towards the industrial building at the base of the pylon. The viewpoint from the top of the hill beneath the pylon was restricted by the edges of the woods. Even with the moon bathing everything in silver, all he could see were trees. He picked his way down the hill, careful not to turn an ankle in the hollows made by the stumps, and found the path to the Split Lane.

The still silence of the night was interrupted periodically by owl hoots and the rustling of small animals in the underbrush nearby. The third or fourth time it happened, he stopped jumping out of his skin, content that any rodent in the bushes beside the path probably wasn't packing a rifle.

He crossed Split Lane from west to east and walked upright along the path that led to the manor house. From the woods beside the lake which sat to the north of the house, he could tell it was bad. The mist rising off the lake framed the mansion, but it had changed, it didn't look right, and as he approached closer, crouching low, he could see why. The four chimneys had collapsed. The strong wooden beams, perpendicular and bold were now missing or pointing skyward when they should have been parallel with the ground. The place was a mess. A burnt-out mess, with the smell of death lingering over it. It was all Marcus could do to keep walking forward, skirting the lake to head to the left of the mansion where the gardens were.

There was no sign of Uncle Reggie or Aunt Meredith, no tent on the lawn or other temporary accommodation, so Marcus hoped that they were somewhere safe, maybe waiting until a better time to come to the bunker and rescue them.

Someone had doused the garden in petrol or other accelerant before setting it alight and then smashing every single pane in the glasshouse. This end of the house seemed relatively intact, so Marcus headed toward the door. From there he could see he was deceived. While the door was missing—totally ripped from its hinges somehow—the hallway beyond was full of rubble from the burnt-out remnants of the incinerated upper floors. Marcus thought of all the food in the butler's pantry. The fridges groaning with food for the guests. The meals that Francine had made for them. His stomach gurgled with the shared fond memory. He turned towards the stables and saw more burnt buildings. The stench wafted gently from that direction and he suddenly felt very sad. He couldn't face what he might find there. He followed the walls of the mansion, trying to see if there was anything untouched inside, if there was any possibility of something to eat. All the while a voice in the back of his head screamed for him to run, to escape, to head back to the bunker. To safety.

He'd worked his way around to the carpark and driveway and noticed that there were two cars awkwardly parked halfway between the gate and the house. The garage had fared no better than the rest of the mansion, with the corpse of the burnt-out Land Rover poking through the debris. The two parked cars were empty.

The only source of food Marcus knew about now was from the fishing lake in the southeast corner of the estate. Without the garage, he didn't know where to find any fishing lines, but he was so hungry that it didn't matter. He decided that even if he had to wade out into the lake and catch the fish with his bare hands and eat it raw he would. He decided not to follow the driveway to the lane down to the corner of the estate, electing to follow the path past the kidney-shaped outdoor swimming pool and beyond through the woods.

The pool also had mist rising off it, looking in the bright moonlight like a set from a horror movie. A zombie emerged from the pool house and lurched towards him. He froze, not believing his eyes. The zombie urgently hissed his name, and he realised it was Ingenue. She beckoned and he followed him back into the pool house. She closed the door and turned to him. "You came for me! Thank you! Did anyone see you?"

"You're welcome," said Marcus, unsure what else to say. "Do you have any food?"

"Uh, no. What's the plan?"

"We've got a bunker up near the cottage. We just need to find some food. The house is burnt down. The cottage is burnt down. The gardens are destroyed. The fishery containers have these mean locks on them and I think there's a guard there. The only thing left is the fishing lake."

"Well, we can't go there: the two guards they posted are down there drinking and night fishing. And we can't go to the neighbours because they're in on it too. Oh, Marcus! Your Uncle! And Aunt! They were taken away."

Marcus made her sit down and tell him what had happened the previous night. She'd been sitting in the library when Uncle Reggie had turned up, yelling. Ingenue couldn't make out the words but the tone made her rush out. William and Francine and Aunt Meredith had all been there and each was given instructions and rushed off. Reggie had placed his hands on her shoulders and told her that some men were coming and that she should hide in the woods, that she wasn't safe here anymore. She'd heard cars screeching to a halt in the carpark and yelling. She fled, getting as far as into the woods on the other side of the lake in front of the house as she could before hearing a group on foot closing in on the house from that direction. She'd hidden and watched as they converged on the house. Yelling was silenced. Petrol cans were produced. Windows were smashed. She watched as flames erupted and burnt the house down. Then in the eerie silence afterwards, punctuated by the collapsing beams and muted explosions of things in the house exploding, some of the cars left. Presumably with Reggie and Meredith inside.

"Did you see the men that took them away? Which cars took them?'

"No, the cars were in the driveway on the other side of the house. And I didn't actually see them getting taken away. I certainly heard yelling though."

"Were there any gunshots?" asked Marcus, wincing in anticipation of her answer.

He couldn't see a frown but could sense her confusion.

"No, why?"

Marcus decided to tell the truth. "They shot the Earl. Or someone at his estate anyway. And they shot at me."

She thought for a minute. "No, no gunshots. The fire burnt for a long time. I slept here in the pool house. Two guys pulled up in cars and wandered around for a while. I was terrified they would find me. Eventually, they headed off towards the fishing lake with some rods. At least I thought they were rods. Maybe they were guns."

Marcus looked around the pool house, wanting for there to be a packet of something to eat lying around, but all there was were pool toys and recliners. "Damn!" he said.

"What's the matter?" Ingenue asked.

"I told Zoe I'd bring her back some food."

"Zoe's your sister? The one who went horse riding?"

"Yeah."

"Well, there's none here," Ingenue said. "Can we go now? I've been scared of being found this whole time. I couldn't sleep with worry. I doze off and then wake up at the tiniest of sounds. I was so relieved when I saw you."

Marcus paused, thinking. There was no food to be had here. Maybe they could go to the Earl's place and search there? Maybe they could find a vacant house with food in it? Maybe they could walk into town and break into a shop in the middle of the night. Maybe. But safety first. Best to get back to the bunker and get some sleep and formulate a plan.

"Sure, let's go." He grabbed an armful of towels from the pile in the corner. "We don't have any blankets," he explained. Ingenue grabbed a couple herself. And then they headed out into the moonlight.

The trip back started quite slowly with Ingenue jumping at each hoot and rustle in the same way that Marcus had done on his way down from the bunker. By the time they reached Split Lane, she had recalibrated what made her stop and freeze in fear. They were part of the way through the woods on the western side of the estate, with the moonlight piercing through the tree canopy to shine on the blanket of blue flowers, when a deer wandered through the glade, pausing to sniff the air before bounding away through the trees. They had been walking upright the whole way, but Marcus made them crouch and dart from shadow to shadow as they approached the top of the hill with the pylon at the top. He was worried about the guard at the shipping containers. He needn't have worried as they made it to the cottage unmolested.

Ingenue slowed, staring at the burnt-out husk of the cottage. She started to talk but stopped at the look of warning on Marcus' face. They negotiated the gate and headed into the pasture. Marcus navigated their way to the entrance to the bunker, waiting a good five minutes with an ear cocked in case they were followed before lifting the door. He sent Ingenue down the steps first, closing the door and letting out a sigh of relief. He squeezed past Ingenue and rapped out the pattern on the door.

The door unlocked and swung open and Zoe's face peered around the edge of it. Her eyes widened as she saw Ingenue in all her bandaged glory. As Marcus led the way inside, he introduced Ingenue and then let Zoe know the bad news. Best she knew straight away.

"There wasn't any food. I found Ingenue though. She was staying at the Mansion. I'll go into town tomorrow night and break into a shop or something for something to eat."

"They burnt down that farmer's house as well!" Ingenue exclaimed. "Why did they do that?"

Marcus could see that she didn't comprehend what had happened. "Ingenue, the whole countryside was on fire last night. That cottage was Uncle Reggie and Aunt Meredith's home. The neighbour's house... the Earl's? Burnt." He angrily locked the door. Zoe was trying to attract his attention. "No, look, sorry, Zoe. I couldn't find any food." He didn't mention the stables.

"Oh! So it wasn't just the Mansion?"

"No, it seems it was a widespread thing. Zoe! What is it?"

"I found something," she said, her eyes gleaming.

"Is it food?" Marcus laughed.

"Come and see," she said, leading the way towards the bathroom.

Ingenue jumped onto the bunk to let him pass. Zoe led him to the cupboard opposite the sink, with the cardboard box in it. He started to explain that he'd already seen the cardboard box when he stopped. She had lifted the box to reveal a hatch on the floor of the bunker. There was no handle or means of opening it that he could see.

"I found a door," she said redundantly. "But I couldn't open it."

Marcus forgot the grumbling in his stomach. A hundred people for a hundred days. It must be the food storage! "You did great, Zoe! Awesome work, now we just need to find a place to put a code." As he said that, he saw that the fuse box about halfway up the wall in the cupboard had a second set of dials beside it. They dials looked exactly like those on the fuse box—the same type of plastic, the same layout. Numbers on moveable rings.

Marcus frowned. OK, so Aunt Meredith's birthday was the code, but what was that? He tried to work out what they'd be told about her birthday party. He recalled it was on the Friday before they arrived, but didn't know if it was actually on her birthday or if it was just shifted to the nearest weekend. And if it was anything like a computer login or unlocking a phone, he'd only get three tries. Better to double-check in case anyone else knew it.

"Zoe, do you remember what Aunt Meredith's birthday was? Ingenue? No?" He spun the dials, pointing to the date of the party, before thinking about the year. Of course, nobody mentioned which birthday it was, that would be rude. And yet here we are with six numbers to find: date and month obviously taking the first four. OK, how old was Uncle Reggie? He was a year older than Mum, so that was a starting point. He placed the dials into position. And then slowly moved them up five places. Nothing. So she wasn't younger than Uncle Reggie. He'd got to the year which would have made Aunt Meredith a year older than Uncle Reggie when he heard a click. The latch didn't open, but he figured something was correct. So maybe that was the year part, and he only now had to figure out the date. He was happy with the month part, and slowly changed the second dial. He was just about to increase the first dial by one when there was a louder click, and the hatch swung open.

THE HOLE: PART TWO

Marcus thought that there should be a golden light streaming out of the hatch with a smorgasbord of pizza and fried chicken at the bottom. Choirs of angels with trumpets playing a fanfare. Instead, there was a ladder heading down a shaft, maybe four feet wide, illuminated by the same fluorescent bulbs and lined with the same industrial white plasterboard as in the bunker. Marcus looked down the shaft and saw that it stopped a mere ten feet below. No food to be seen.

"Uncle Reggie said that there was food in the bunker and this seems to be the only place it could be. I'd say collect your belongings and let's go, but we don't have anything, so let's just go. Zoe, do you want to come down after me? Ingenue, are you ok bringing up the rear?" He started to climb down the rungs, trying to temper his expectations. The last thing he wanted was to fixate on a feast and then find nothing.

The bunker had seemed to be brand new, maybe not fully completed with the disconnected TV and gas bottles. The stitching on the mattresses didn't show any signs of wear and the walls were clean and unblemished. Unlived in, guessed Marcus. And that feeling continued into the tunnel leading down. A box on the wall at the bottom of the ladder held a similar combination lock as they'd found in the cupboard, and the chamber they found themselves in was freshly lined with the same boards as above. The similarity stopped at the opening from the chamber.

A natural cavern ran away from it, a line of light bulbs dangling from a single white power line attached by metal hooks driven into the wall or ceiling. The ceiling and floor were both uneven, the distance between them looking to average out at a good ten feet from Marcus's vantage point at the head of the corridor. He could smell the night even down here, which suggested that there was some sort of opening into the outside world—or maybe the scent had come with them through the bunker upstairs. There was no sign of moisture on the stone walls or floor, and the ceiling seemed free of damp also. Steeling himself, Marcus led the way down into the cavern.

The single bare bulbs were spaced twenty metres apart. Occasionally, a bulb was blown, making a shadowy area where they'd stumble and curse as they grazed their shins or bumped their knees in the dark. Marcus hadn't seen the bulbs flicker on and wondered if they stayed on the whole time and how they were powered. A battery? Connected to the mains somehow?

They settled into their trek, their breathing and occasional grunts the only sounds in the tunnel. It was relatively straight, so they could frequently see the line of bulbs stretching out in front of them, the missing bulbs standing out as some sort of weird morse code. Dot-dot-dot-dot-dash-dot-dot... It was when this pattern suddenly stopped that they realised they were coming to the end of the corridor. They'd been walking about half an hour. The final bulb brought them up to a metal door set into a solid stone dead end. Whereas the bunker's doors and hatches had been white-painted metal and sized for humans, the new door in the tunnel was only half that height and constructed of an old and heavy-looking metal, unpainted but unrusted—more of a hatch than a door, with a hinge at the top and a horizontal handle halfway up.

When they were all near, Marcus waited for them to indicate that they were ready and then planted his feet and lifted the handle. The hatch opened easily, some sort of counter-weight helping him lift the heavy metal. On the other side was a compact round tunnel lined with corrugated iron, its floor lined with empty hessian sacks. The tunnel itself took a tight turn to the right, disappearing into darkness. Marcus asked Zoe for the phone—it didn't have a torch app, but the glow of the screen was something—and got on his hands and knees, one hand outstretched in front with the phone, the other on the floor for support. Inch by inch, he made his way along the tunnel. It stopped in a closet. A literal closet. The phone glow illuminated the inside of the door. There was a light switch beside it. The ceiling in the closet was normal height and so Marcus stood, noticing that the closet had coat hangers hanging from a rod at eye level, but there were no clothes anywhere. He flicked on the light switch and cursed as he was blinded by the light. He could hear the others making their way along the short, corrugated iron tunnel to join him so he opened the door, not wanting to be crammed inside the closet with two others.

He stood in a bedroom with a double bed. Beside the closet door, an open door spilled light into an en suite and a closed door faced him. The room was carpeted and looked like a normal room in any residential house, except that there were no personal effects around or pictures on the walls. The bed wasn't made up—rather, a large plastic bag filled with brand new sheets, blankets and pillows, still in their original plastic wrapping, sat at the end of the mattress. The mattress wasn't a faceless industrial model like in their original bunker. This one had a brand name and, judging by the label still embroidered into the fabric, was a King-Sized Super Firm. He flicked the room lights on and turned to wait for the others to enter.

"Stay close. We don't know if anyone else is in here," Marcus told them, listening at the door. All he could hear was his own pulse thudding in his ears, so he shrugged and opened the door. He was in a corridor with wooden floorboards and fluorescent lighting automatically flicking itself on via movement detection. His was one of four doors leading off the corridor, two per side, and the corridor itself ended ten feet away in a door of its own.

He ignored the other three doors closest to him and walked to the end of the corridor. He knew from video games and movies that he should be checking each room as they went by to make sure there were no enemies behind them—to allow for a clear escape path back through to the tunnel—but his brain had been fixed on the fact that if there was a bedroom, there would have to be a kitchen and if there was a kitchen then there might be food. And if there were four bedrooms, then any kitchen should have four times as much food as if there'd been just one. So he wasted no time in getting to the end of the corridor and opening the door.

Beyond the door was a great space. Great by the standards of the bunker, anyway. As the fluorescent lights flickered on, he got a piecemeal view of the room. It was about twice the size of the bedroom, a combination lounge/kitchen area with doors between the fridge and the oven in the kitchen and at the opposite end, between the two couches in the lounge, was a large plasma screen TV. It would have cost a fortune ten years ago. On the table in front of the TV, sat a remote and a computer keyboard. On a bookshelf surrounding the TV was a collection of tablets of different sizes, plus assorted manuals.

Marcus ignored all these and made his way swiftly into the kitchen area. There was a dining table for eight, plus two seats at a breakfast bar at the end of the bench. Brand new appliances sat on the benches and the stickers and plastic wrapping were still on the oven and microwave. It looked as if someone had raided a homeware store, installed everything then been called away before making the kitchen area truly ready for the owner. Marcus flung open the fridge. Nothing. He rummaged through the drawers and cupboards in the kitchen. Brand new pots and pans, cutlery, tea towels. But no food. He let out an expletive. He heard Ingenue's voice nearby. "In here!"

Zoe and Ingenue were standing in the doorway between the stove and the fridge, staring in wonder at the shelves which lined the walls of the room. The shelving was seven levels deep in parts, populated with various large buckets and plastic boxes. He read one of the labels. "Emergency Food: 30 day, 1 person kit. 2000 calories." There were many different brands of kit, in different sizes, all laid out on shelves perfectly sized for each container height.

Marcus was awestruck. "Food for a hundred people for a hundred days!"

He grabbed the closest box and ripped it open. Six large cans of... powdered scrambled eggs? Zoe nudged his leg. She was sitting on the floor surrounded by small packages, the contents of a pack she'd split open. She had some sort of chocolate bar crammed in her mouth and was handing him a packet of crackers with a tube that purported to contain strawberry jam. Behind her, Ingenue was helping herself to another of the packs. Marcus barely paused to squirt a swirl of jam on the crackers before trying to fit the whole thing in his mouth at once.

An impressive display of gluttony then ensued, the contents of the packages quickly disappearing as they discovered things that could be eaten immediately. Anything that required cooking ended up on the floor. By the end of it, they were all lying down, slumped in a line, their backs against the shelving and the carnage of wrappers and crumbs surrounding them. Zoe looked like an off-brand clown, with a ring of chocolate around her mouth. Ingenue's white dressing gown and facial bandages were covered in powdered soup from where the packet had opened unexpectedly easily, exploding in a hilarious cloud of chicken flavouring. Marcus's shirt now had rivulets of jam dripping down its front. The packs they'd opened had included tubes of condensed milk and the sweet liquid had quenched thirst as well as satisfying caloric deficiency. But they still needed water.

Marcus started to collect the wrappers and put them in the containers that they had come from. It took no time at all and on the way back into the kitchen they found some glasses in the dark wood cupboards and slaked their thirst from the tap. He took the opportunity to wipe Zoe's face with a brand new cloth he had found under the sink and was about to hand it to Ingenue before realising that it wouldn't help her with the soup.

The only place they hadn't investigated was through the last door in the lounge. Marcus figured it must lead to the outside world—after all, how else would the owners of the bunker be able to get in? He opened the door and looked through, flicking on the light switch just inside the door.

The room beyond was about the size of the bedroom whose closet they'd arrived in, with a super vault door opposite Marcus's door to the lounge and a bathroom through a doorway to the right. The vault door impressed with a huge wheel in the middle of it and a sliding slot at eye level. Marcus walked over and slid the slot across. Ahead of him, the corridor disappeared into the darkness, with just a suggestion of steps leading upwards. The left-hand switch beside the door lit up the corridor and confirmed that it ended in the steps rising up to a door in the ceiling. The others had followed him in and Ingenue announced from the bathroom that it had a shower in it as well. Zoe came over and insisted on being lifted up to see through the slot, and Marcus obliged.

"Where does that go?' she asked, referring to the hatch above the stairs.

Marcus looked at Ingenue in case she had followed the twists and turns underground and had any idea of where they were. She shook her head. "I've got no idea, Zoe," he answered. "But I guess we should find out." He looked at the phone. 4:30 am. If he popped up someplace public, he should be ok - surely nobody would be out and about this late? Or was it early?

He turned to Ingenue. "Could you look after the door, in case I have to come running back? We might have to shut it in a hurry."

She nodded, and they spent a few minutes figuring out how to operate it. It was pretty simple. The wheel in the middle of the door drove locking pins into the door jam. Big heavy locking pins. Turning the wheel the other way retracted the locking pins. Marcus was now starting to feel a little tired. He had slipped a little into the same mentality he had when he was playing an exploration game on the computer—just one more turn to explore the map, to see what was out there, to complete the mental picture of where he was. Of what was around. He walked down the corridor and climbed the steps. The steps and corridor reminded him that this bunker seemed totally different from the one at the Cottage. Whereas that one had seemed new and a little antiseptic, this one, although also unlived in, had been set up to be homely and welcoming. Hence the wood panelling in the kitchen cupboards, the carpeting of the floors and the skirting boards around the edges of the walls. The inside of the hatch didn't even have a latch, just a metal bar allowing you to pull it closed. Marcus tried to open it, but it wouldn't budge. It moved maybe an inch but something was blocking it on the other side. The inch allowed a brief shower of ash to come inside and all of a sudden the stench of stale smoke filled the corridor. Marcus had an idea of where they'd ended up, but headed back to the others, lost in thought.

"Why didn't you go through?" Zoe asked as he came back into the room. Marcus made sure the door was completely locked before he answered.

"I couldn't budge the door. It was blocked on the other side. I could smell old burning though."

"What, like a fireplace? Who would have a fire now? It's summer."

Marcus smiled at Zoe. "More like the leftovers of a house fire. Like the Earl's mansion. And Uncle Reggie and Aunt Meredith's."

Ingenue realised what he was saying. "So you're saying I've walked from the mansion to the bunker twice over - once over ground and once underground?"

"I think so," Marcus replied. "The way I figure it, we're pretty safe here. We've got enough food, we've got a main entrance which seems to be secure with the outer door blocked and then this massive door as well. We have the other bunker which has a locked door and hidden entrance. Plus the secret hatch with a passcode."

"So we just sit here and wait to be rescued?" asked Ingenue.

"Well, I'm not sure who will be coming. And where will they go to rescue us? The same things which keep us safe make us impossible to rescue. And we don't know what is going on in the outside world. I can go for a scout at night. Maybe steal a newspaper or something to find out what's going on."

Ingenue nodded slowly. "And if anyone was going to use the bunker they would not be able to anyway, so we're not taking food away from anyone else, right?"

"Right. I guess we should check out the bedroom situation: I'm beat!"

They headed back to the living quarters, pausing briefly to check out each of the other three rooms and finding them identically laid out with the exception of the passage in the closet.

Ingenue selected one of the other rooms: "I know that it should be safe, but I don't think that I would be able to sleep knowing that the closet opens out to the rest of the world."

Marcus agreed and selected the room next to hers for himself and Zoe. "Unless you want a room of your own?" Zoe shook her head, smiling. "OK, see if there are towels and soap for a shower: I'll make up the bed." He had only just opened the packaging of the first set of sheets when a squeal from the bathroom sent him straight there. Zoe was crouching on the floor beside wide open cupboards under the sink.

"Look at all the toothbrushes! And soaps! And shampoo!" she said, delightedly pointing. Marcus bent down and looked inside. On the left were two full sets of towels tied together with a bow. On the right-hand side was box after box of toothbrushes. Beside these were dozens and dozens of the small soaps and bottles of shampoo that Marcus had seen in hotels on TV and in movies. On the shelf below them were two robes and two plastic bags with slippers in them.

"Only take one out, Zoe." Marcus went back to making up the bed. He listened to Zoe getting one of everything off the shelves while putting the fitted sheet on the bed, getting it around the wrong way at first, before putting the duvet into its cover. He heard the shower turn on. And a little while later a pensive voice rang out, complaining that there was no hot water. He headed in to find Zoe wearing the robe and slippers, with her clothes strewn across the room and one hand testing the water.

"Oh, no, it's starting to get warm now," she corrected herself. "That took a while!" Marcus headed back again to finish putting the pillowcases onto the pillows, placing all the packaging into the original large plastic bag which had held everything and sliding it into the closet.

By the time he'd brushed his teeth and had a shower himself, Zoe was in bed asleep. Marcus resented having to put his dirty underwear and T-shirt back on but resolved to wash everything in the sink the next day.

WAITING

He woke in the dark. Alone. He got up and put his grubby jeans back on and then headed out to the lounge. Zoe was watching Ingenue cook something on the stove while keeping up a pretty one-sided conversation. They both turned as he approached and said Good Morning.

"What's for breakfast?"

"Ingenue made scrambled eggs!"

"Marcus, do you want to grab some plates? Zoe, you get some glasses of water and hop up to the table."

Over breakfast, they laid out a plan. They'd check the phones for each of the saved numbers plus the police numbers every second day. That should keep the battery fresh enough in case the phone system magically started working. They'd check out the TV to see if it had any news channels or the internet could fill in what was going on in the outside world. Ingenue mentioned she had to do a set number of exercises and Zoe mentioned that she'd do them too. The bandages were looking a little worse for wear and Ingenue agreed that they'd have to come off soon. A couple of days early, but if they found a first aid kit, she could always replace them.

Zoe asked if it was to stop the bleeding, that being her only frame of reference for injuries and wounds.

"More to keep the swelling down, I think," responded Ingenue.

They tidied up the breakfast dishes and then headed to the lounge. Marcus made a big ceremony of checking the phones, but the results were the same as they had been previously.

The keyboard on the coffee table in front of the TV turned out to be wireless and after turning on the TV they saw a menu system featuring movie after movie and whole series of TV programs, all organised into folders and subfolders. The tablets on the shelves turned out to be old iPads, unlocked with only the built-in programs and the Kindle App. The library was equally impressive, with title after title of books to choose from. But the piece de resistance was one of the ring-bound folders. As soon as he started to read it, Marcus knew what it was and bid the others to sit down while he read out what it said.

"Welcome to the BunkMaster 4000. The BM4000 contains everything you will need for a comfortable stay for 10,000 days. The BM4000 includes four of our BR100 double en-suite bedroom units which sleep two people, our KL200 open plan lounge/kitchen unit with optional storage room and a SE900 secure entrance system. The KL200 includes a full media library of one hundred terabytes of movies, TV programs and books and manuals to keep you entertained, and the included food, water and power package will allow you to maintain the same standard of living as you enjoyed previously. You can also upgrade at a very reasonable price to our SS750 expansion which includes hydroponic farming, a water reclamation system and alternate power supplies which make the BM4000 truly self-sustaining and will support an indefinite stay. Other optional upgrades include the SS850 which includes satellite dish and internet connectivity." The next page listed all the things included in the standard package: each of the meal parcels, the flavours and calories and how long they'd last. The toiletries and cleaning supplies. Page after page of descriptions of what one person might need for 10,000 days, or two people for 5,000 days, or three people for 3,333 days. Which, Marcus mentally calculated, meant that in theory they could stay down here for a little over 9 years. If the place was full to capacity, with two people per bedroom, then that would mean they could only stay down for 1250 days, or three and a bit years.

"What's hydro... hydrophonics?" asked Zoe.

"Hydroponics is when you grow plants in water," said Ingenue. "I had a boyfriend who grew... plants like that. Apparently, it's very effective. Anyways, I have to do some exercises, so I'm going to go into the 'SE900' and do them there."

"Can I come too?" asked Zoe, looking up at Ingenue.

Ingenue looked over at Marcus who shrugged.

"Sure, come on. I'll teach you. It's fun!"

Marcus settled down in front of the TV and tried to see if there were any hidden menu items that might hide an internet browser or something unrelated to the movies and TV programs on the media centre. When that came up empty, he tried weird and wonderful combinations of key presses to see if he could circumvent the menu system and access the computer that must be running it. Nothing.

Then he decided to try and find the computer hardware. That at least he was partially successful at, tracing the wires from the TV down the back of the cupboard into a hole in the wall. It was also where the power cable went. So somewhere behind the wall was a computer, which may or may not have a connection to the internet.

Marcus had a thought. The iPads would surely show all the network connections available in the room. So, as long as any internet connection was attached to a wireless router, he should at least be able to see the connection, even if he couldn't connect to it.

A brief examination showed that the only connection available was to "MediaCentre", which just meant that they could connect to the computer running the TVs and movies. It didn't mean that the MediaCentre definitely wasn't connected to the internet and therefore the outside world, it just meant that it was highly unlikely. Any connection would need to be wired. And, from what he'd seen, this bunker was made to be detached from the world in every possible way.

He thought it pertinent to read something about someone in a similar situation to himself, and so chose Anne Frank's Diary from Kindle on one of the iPads and made himself comfortable on the couch. He was so engrossed that he didn't hear Zoe and Ingenue come back from their exercises and head for the showers. Nor even when they came back and chatted quietly in the kitchen.

It wasn't until Zoe picked out an iPad of her own and clambered onto the couch beside him that he registered that they were both in the room. Ingenue took the other couch. She shifted uncomfortably.

"Hey, I was thinking about something and I don't know what it means, but thought I'd run it past you."

"Sure, shoot."

"I don't think your Uncle made this bunker. Or bought it."

"What do you mean?"

"How long has he owned the estate?"

"I think he's had it something like five years, maybe a little less."

"There's also the difference in newness between the other bunker and this one," she continued. "Who has a plasma TV nowadays? Everything is LCD or LED. The iPads are almost ten years old. I think this bunker was from the previous owners—those short people from the book you were reading."

Marcus frowned as he considered this. He nodded, it made sense. "Good points, but what does it mean? Should we be looking for guns or drugs?"

It was Ingenue's turn to frown. "I'm not sure. I haven't figured that bit out yet. I guess it means that if your Uncle comes back, he might not know about this place. Otherwise, he'd surely have escaped here himself with everyone from the house, right?"

Marcus looked around the bunker. "But he specifically told me about the food, so he must have known about it... Surely? Are you saying that we should wait for him in the other bunker?" The unspoken part of the sentence was "without bedding, showers or food".

Ingenue shook her head. "As I said, I haven't thought it through. It would be good if we had some sort of security camera system to keep an eye on the other bunker or, even better still, to keep an eye out on the outside world. But I don't think there is one."

Marcus thought of the drones which had caught the poachers. It would be great to have access to them. They'd be able to figure out what was going on and not be seen themselves. Perfect! But if this bunker system predated Uncle Reggie, and he didn't know about it, then there was zero chance it was somehow connected to the drone system. Damn.

Ingenue got up and returned with her own iPad. "Just a thought," she said. "As I said, I don't know what it means."

Marcus smiled at her and nodded, turning back to his book.

Time in the bunker had a consistency all of its own. It slipped by effortlessly while he was reading, but was glacially slow otherwise. Without the sun, they were governed by their stomachs and sleepiness. About 6 pm they selected their evening meal from the list in the manual and then headed into the larder to hunt down the brand and type of package they'd selected. Much easier than trying to look through the packages for something good because they all looked the same from the outside. They cooked the parts of the package that needed heating and shared what they had, using it as a trial of the different flavours. Marcus noticed that Ingenue only actually ate half the rations—her diet of a thousand calories a day conveniently half the amount of each of the servings.

Marcus wasn't sure how long they'd been down in the bunker by the time the sunless routine was finally broken. They had food, they had water, they could stay clean and they had things to do, so although they were wholly and totally disconnected from the rest of the world, they were existing and they felt safe. They finished dinner and cleaned up afterwards, talking a bit about each of the books they were reading. Ingenue had mentioned that she would do a load of washing and Marcus leapt at the chance to have clean clothes to put on after a shower. So they all trekked to their rooms and changed into dressing gowns and slippers and passed Ingenue their clothes. She put the load into the washing machine which was beside the dishwasher under the sink in the kitchen. They then retired to the lounge and watched a zombie movie on the big screen, stopping halfway through to attend to the washing.

After humanity had been saved and the credits were rolling, Ingenue chortled and turned to Marcus. "My agent is an older guy—real straight shooter. Has a hilarious turn of phrase, very entertaining. Anyways, he has a cynical take on why zombie movies are so popular. He reckons the current generation is arrogant. That they want to be the ones who fuck everything up. To destroy society. He reckons it's a continuation of all the doomsday cults and fundamental religions waiting for the rapture too. What's so special about our era? Why would the world end just because we're here to see it? What's so special about us?" She looked around at their surroundings. "Pretty funny now, when you think about it."

Marcus shared her wry grin. "You don't think it's wish fulfilment? The only way the less attractive guys can get the pretty girls? 'I wouldn't go out with you if you were the last man on the earth'. 'What about now?'"

Ingenue laughed at that. "And why do they all have sniper's rifles?"

"Campers." Marcus snorted dismissively.

"Campers?"

"In computer games—first-person shooters—there's a type of player who finds a nice little hidey-hole and just snipes from cover. The worst ones set up so they can shoot you when you come back into the game and so there's a bottleneck and they just pick you off as soon as you come back. So they're 'camping at the respawn spot' or camping. Thus 'campers'. Not quite cheating but pretty shitty. So in the zombie apocalypse it's an attractive idea to hide somewhere and pick your enemies off from a distance so you're not exposed."

Ingenue nodded. "The funniest part is that Americans think the world will be overridden by zombies. They haven't been to Europe obviously."

Marcus didn't get it. "I don't get it, what do you mean?" he asked.

Ingenue explained. "So cities in the US are these huge square blocks of buildings separated by wide roads and then connected to others by huge freeways across farmland, right? Impossible to defend."

Marcus nodded. "Yeah, with you so far."

"But in England, and on the continent you have cities that were created for protection. That have stood up to siege and conflict and are therefore perfect for holding off a zombie horde."

"But what if the occupants are all turned."

"So if you can make it to the walls, you're fine. Two people back-to-back, with anything they can use as a shield, bash the zombies that are on the wall so they get knocked off. You clear the walls first and close the gates. Now you have a perimeter, so you get a spear and stand at the top of the stairs to the walls and poke them in the head, while your partner holds up the shield. Clear out the interior and the stone walls which have held up against centuries of invaders keep you safe. The shield wall has been a great defensive tactic since before the Romans. And if you have an iron gate you can put a couple of kids with spears behind it and they'll happily poke the zeds in the head until the sun goes down."

"But what if the zombies are like the speedy ones in World War Z?"

"Oh, then you're fucked. But if they're like that then you're fucked no matter what you do."

"Well, what about restarting society? In Europe I mean?"

"If it's possible to reuse cities in Europe, then the zombie outbreak will be put down quicker, there will be less societal change, less starting from zero and therefore it won't take as long to get back to a semblance of normal.

It'll be quicker to get some technology into the picture: a machine like a giant lawnmower turned upside down with a siren in the middle to attract the zeds. Keeps going until it runs out of gas or gets clogged up. Unmanned so perfectly safe. A concrete trench filled with petrol that's on fire, like a moat."

"Wait, why would the zombies go into the moat?"

"Well, you could put some plastic wrap near the edges and soap it up until it's slippery. One thing zombies aren't is agile. They'd hit the slide, whooomph! Fried zed before they knew what was happening!"

"Or some industrial drones with no blade protection. Thwip!"

"Yeah, so I guess the difference between cities in America and Europe is that the ones in Europe were built for protection—people came together for protection over the centuries. Funny though, even protected by stone walls, nature can triumph over Man. Our French class went to Paris for a week, to brush up our language skills, and when we were in the Louvre our guide told us about a pack of wolves that preyed on the citizens of Paris. The winter had been pretty desolate so the starving pack of wolves came closer and closer to the outskirts of Paris. The city walls were in disrepair, so even though the woods nearby had been chopped down for firewood, the wolves gained access to the city and roamed the streets, killing the peasant folk by night and hiding out by day. Eventually, the Parisians had enough and banded together and drove the wolves onto the Isle de Cite in front of Notre Dame and slaughtered them there. Again, a large enough group of untrained peasants with spears can keep a mass of wolves... or zombies, in check."

"Wow, lucky you—going to Paris for school. Furthest we got was class camp on Motutapu Island. Nobody speaks French there."

Ingenue looked surprised. "Oh, lots of schools send a class to Paris. The school doesn't have to be posh."

Marcus thought for a bit, looking at Zoe who had fallen asleep on the couch. "Next, you'll be telling me that everyone has a horse over here too?"

"Owning a horse? Yeah, that's only the well-to-do. But riding horses? Yeah, anyone can do that."

"I wonder if the Earl had horses." He recalled the smell of smoke, the view across to the Earl's mansion from the hill. The echo of the gunshot. "The Earl hadn't actually done anything wrong, had he?"

"Hard to blame someone for having rich parents, right?"

"And Uncle Reggie certainly hadn't done anything wrong."

"I guess it's not really them that were being attacked then? The Earl was just a symbol of wealth that's locked up in a family for centuries."

"And Uncle Reggie? What was he a symbol of?"

Ingenue was quiet for a while, thinking. "I guess he was in the wrong place at the wrong time. And if all the people with 'hand-me-down wealth' all live in the big houses, then if you attack the big houses you're going to get some self-made people caught up in the mayhem. I think when people get that backed into a corner they lash out and sometimes hurt people that they don't mean to."

"I don't know, the guys chasing us across the farm seemed to mean it."

"And if you tried to argue the point, you probably would have ended up the same as the Earl. Mobs aren't known for their debating skills, or their receptiveness to sound arguments."

"It's just frustrating that we aren't posh and yet they're shooting us. Sure Uncle Reggie is doing alright, but..."

"Yeah, but from their point of view, there's nothing different separating you from the rich folk. When you're born, you roll the dice. From their point of view, you're one of those who rolled a six. While they rolled a one. And it's harder and harder to change your lot. Sixes stay sixes. Ones stay ones."

"Do ones always stay ones? Can you be successful if your parents weren't?"

"Your man Goodacre didn't seem to be able to improve his life from what his ancestors had enjoyed. Besides, what's success?"

Marcus snorted. "Good point. I guess I define that as 'doing better than my parents'."

"Right, so I guess the question then is - how many people do better than their parents?"

"Well, you don't want to equate that with how much you get paid surely? There are heaps of stories about how the rich are really miserable."

"I don't know if you can take any notice of that—sure, money can't buy happiness, but you can at least be miserable in comfort, right?"

Marcus thought for a while. "I guess what I like about New Zealand is that even if you weren't born into money, I think you can make things better for yourself. Sure, that's easier for me than for some of my friends. But compared with some other countries..."

"Like here?"

"I don't know. New Zealand hasn't just had an armed uprising to kill the rich, so maybe we're a little better at making sure people have opportunity. But I've been in this country for five minutes and seen one city and one estate. What do I know about a hundred million people's individual experiences?"

They were quiet for a while after that, Marcus watching Zoe breathing. Thinking. Ingenue broke the silence.

"You're very good with her."

"Who, Zoe? She's alright. Lots of practice. When Mum and Dad split, Mum was away a lot at work to all hours. First, my older brother looked after us both and then he'd be away at his job, or at school and so it would be just me and her."

"No horses at home?"

"No, and don't remind her of the horses. I'm scared of what happened to them. There was a terrible smell from the stables after the fire."

"I think the horses got away. I heard a commotion when I was hiding in the woods and saw a bunch of them disappearing down the driveway. Just the heads bobbing up and down over the top of the hedges. I don't know where they ended up, but I don't think they were in the stables."

Marcus's face was the picture of relief.

"It's funny how owning a horse is the benchmark for being well off, right?" Ingenue continued. "Nobody in my neighbourhood had horses either. We weren't poor, just your normal suburban family. Dad's mum had a bit of money and left me and my brother a little bit when she passed away. He went to Bali with some mates for his gap year. And I did this," she indicated the bandages which were now only very loosely covering her head, collecting on her shoulders like a scarf. "I was getting close to getting some really good roles, the last three sort of thing for some movie roles—and they don't come up too often in England. So, my agent had a quiet word with the casting people and tried to find out what was holding me back. Was my nose too big, was I too fat, too skinny, butt too big, tits too small?"

"Isn't it what's inside that supposed to count?"

Ingenue paused for a second, obviously seeing if he was being serious. Finally deciding to take him at face value. "In real life, yes. But actors don't live in real life, they live in casting rooms and on sets and if they're lucky on red carpets or podiums accepting awards. So, if ten casting directors all say the same thing, and you've got the money, and your agent thinks it'll get you from being third runner up to being the starring lady, you think... why not? Oh, by the way, if we get out of here, I didn't get any work done, right? I was only on holiday at the mansion."

Marcus nodded in agreement. "Sure. So which was it? The nose, the belly, the butt or the boobs?" he asked with a laugh.

Ingenue's voice had a resigned tone. "All of the above. I don't know if I'll recognise myself when I take the bandages off. And I'm really scared that all of this," she gestured at the bunker, "has put a spanner in the works.

That's a lot of money and pain down the sink if it doesn't work." She seemed to collect herself. "And what about you, Marcus, what's home like for you? Do you enjoy school?"

Marcus thought for a bit. "So we definitely aren't in a horse-owning area. You know what an inorganic collection is? It's when you put out all your garbage that doesn't go in your standard weekly collection and the council comes and collects it. So the footpaths are covered with all sorts of things: old fridges, car bodies, metal swing sets, broken TVs—you name it. Scrap metal guys go cruising along to see if there's anything they can make a dollar off. Anyways, the joke we tell is that if people in a rich neighbourhood have things stolen from their place, then they should come through our neighbourhood during the inorganic and they should be able to find it there. Unfortunately, it's not only the rich getting robbed. We had a couple of break-ins and there's always people trying to take your stuff off you on the streets. Let's just say that you learn not to be too flashy or show off what you've got."

"And what about school?"

"I do OK. I like computers. I made my own one at home. I want to be a programmer when I..."

"...grow up?" Ingenue finished for him. She looked him up and down. "You are tall! The girls must love you!"

Marcus could feel himself blushing. "Uh, I don't know about that," he stammered. "I find it hard to know what to say to girls."

"You don't seem to have any trouble talking to me."

"Yeah, but you're not a ..."

"I assure you that I most definitely am a girl, Marcus!" said Ingenue, mock-outraged.

"But with the bandages, I guess I can focus on what you say."

Ingenue nodded slowly. "I guess that makes sense. How long do you think we'll be stuck in here? Please don't say 10,000 days. I don't think I could stand to be here for twenty years."

Marcus smiled. "Well, Ann Frank was in her hideaway for a bit over two years, before she was found."

"Yeah, but it's nothing like that. They had to get food from outside and we're self-sufficient. And I don't think many people know we're here, so unless we do something stupid I think we should be ok."

"They reckon that somebody in their support network might have dobbed them in."

"We did Ann Frank in school. The teacher asked the class if they would have helped the Jews. Everybody put their hands up. It's easy to judge after the fact, but when it's your life on the line as well, how much are you really going to risk? And then in Drama we read 12 Years A Slave. And the teacher asked the class who would have helped the underground railroad, smuggling escaped slaves from the South to the North where they could be free. We had an African American exchange student who was trying to get into RADA, and he looked at all the hands in the air and commented that if this many people had supported the underground railroad, then it wouldn't have had to be underground. It's easy to say the right things in the safety of today, but when it's your life on the line, would you do the right thing? Would you go over and above?" She was silent for a long time. "I don't know that we can bank on anyone helping us."

Marcus nodded sagely. "Well it might not be two years like Ann Frank, but it'll only be until our flight home, surely?"

Her silence seemed savage.

"I guess... but do you have your passports? Your tickets? Are flights still running? Is anyone looking for you by name? Will you be rounded up by the local version of the Gestapo? And would you abandon me?"

"I haven't thought this through. There's just so much that we don't know. If only we could see what was going on out there, we could figure out what would work and what wouldn't. And if they're looking for just me or you as well. I mean, me and Zoe stand out. If anyone is looking for a tall boy, er, young man and a young girl, we match that description. And especially if they know what we look like. But you...." Marcus froze. An inkling had exploded in his mind. "Um... Ingenue... does anyone at the mansion know what you look like?"

THE PLAN

Ingenue got his point straight away. "Oh my god, you're right! Nobody knows what I look like! So even if they're looking for me as long as I'm not wearing bandages or a dressing gown, I should be fine. The booking at the hotel was in the name of my agent, so there's nothing tying me to the patient who escaped."

"Let's think this through. If you snuck out and walked into town, found a newsagent and looked for newspapers you might be able to read about what's going on. If we had any money you might be able to buy one and then we could figure it out."

"Just playing devil's advocate here, but what if there are no newspapers? What if I say something wrong to people and give us away?"

Marcus thought for a while. 'I don't know if the people working for Uncle Reggie would be loyal or not. But I guess if you can't find William or Francine at the house, then the next person to talk to might be the guy from the Duck's Bark."

"The Duck's Bark?"

"It's a pub. A gastropub. I don't know where it is but surely you won't get in trouble for asking someone for directions?"

"You don't know where it is?"

"I've been there once, but we were driven there. I can tell you it's to the west of the estate, but I couldn't give you directions without being there to recognise the landmarks."

"Ah ok, and who is the guy there?"

"Uh... " Marcus racked his brain. He could picture him, holding court from behind the bar. "He owns the place. Robert, I think his name is."

"And what do I tell him? How do I find out if he's on our side?"

"You could say 'Terrible what happened at Eastwell Manor, isn't it?' If he agrees, then he might be on our side, but if he says 'no' or 'what do you mean?', you can say that it's terrible that Uncle Reggie got taken away. Rather than being shot."

"I don't know, sounds dangerous."

Marcus smiled. "Sounds like a good role to me. A good test of your improv skills."

Ingenue nodded and sounded rueful. "And instead of a bad review..."

"Think positively! Awards for getting it right!"

"Hmmm.... Should I go at night so I can slip away? Or should I go during the day in case there's a curfew? Should I go straight away? Or should we wait for a bit?"

Marcus thought for a bit. If Ingenue's life was resting on the results of their thinking it would be a good idea to consider everything. "What are you going to wear?"

"Huh?" Ingenue managed.

"A dressing gown screams 'mental hospital escapee'. Is that the look we're going for here?"

"That's a good point," agreed Ingenue. And then after another pause: "Did the manual mention a sewing machine?"

Marcus checked it out and towards the end between scrubbing brushes x20 and shoe shine (black) x10 was a reference to sewing kits. "There are supposed to be some, but where would we find them?"

"It's getting late, we'll have a look tomorrow. And decide when I should go."

"And whether you want me to come along and hide in the bushes. You never know when you'll need back up."

"Maybe. Do you need a hand with Zoe?"

"Nah, I'll be ok. She's very light. Good night!" He picked Zoe up and carried her to the room, depositing her gently on the bed. Even though he was tired, he made sure to brush his teeth, leaving the light off in the bedroom so Zoe wasn't disturbed. He climbed into bed and tried to sleep. The room was totally dark and it wasn't long before he fell into a deep slumber.

He woke up and tried to remember his dream. He'd been in an airport and had had to give his bag to a staff member who placed it on the other side of a door which only the staff member was allowed through, beckoning for Marcus to go through a door further along the wall. It was a foreign airport and so all communication was in gestures and grunts for some reason. By the time Marcus reached the door, he was allowed through. The corridor on the other side was filled with some sort of school group, flowing along and preventing him from walking the small distance back to where the other door was and, more importantly, to his bag. His salmon-like struggles had woken him. Zoe had already got up.

He headed out to the lounge, checking the time on the phone which he kept in his dressing gown pocket. It was 9 am—he was surprised but the result of a late night and the lack of any natural light or alarm was that he'd slept later than he normally did. Zoe— sitting on the floor rather than on the couch—was watching a cartoon on the big screen TV, the sound thankfully low, her neck craned at an unusual angle to take in the picture, like sitting in the front row at the cinema.

He grunted a good morning at her then headed to the kitchen and rustled up some more eggs, cooking a whole bucket of powdered scrambled eggs which was supposed to feed eight. He served up three plates and hunted down a plastic container for the remainder. He took Zoe hers and she ate it without her eyes leaving the big screen. He wondered if he should take

Ingenue her breakfast but couldn't decide whether that would be intrusive, so elected to leave it on the bench and cleaned up after himself.

Ingenue emerged not long after, yawning a greeting.

"I made eggs," he said. She smiled her thanks and ate at the table. He joined her and they spoke in hushed tones.

"I think I can convert the duvet cover from one of the spare rooms into a dress which might be presentable," she said.

"Can you sew?" he asked.

"I helped with costumes in the local theatre groups," she said. "It's a great way to keep front of mind with directors and casting folk when you don't get a role in that year's play. And it can't hurt if you make the main character's dress fit you perfectly when you're the understudy!"

"How long do you think it'll take?"

"Well, normally I'd say two or three days, but the duvet cover already has a seam down the sides, so one, maybe two days? I don't have any shoes though. What size are you?"

It turned out that neither Marcus's nor Zoe's shoes would fit, so after breakfast Ingenue disappeared back into her bedroom with a couple of the sewing kits that had been discovered in the corner of the larder. Marcus joined Zoe after her cartoon had finished and they watched a kids movie. This took them to lunch, which Zoe helped Marcus prepare. He delivered the beef-flavoured noodles accompanied by crackers and a tube of cheese spread, and when he came back Zoe asked what Ingenue was doing.

"We need to find out what is going on out in the world," Marcus explained. "We've got to figure out what happened with Aunt Meredith and Uncle Reggie and how we're going to get home. So Ingenue is making a dress so that she can go out to that pub we ate at and ask the owner if he knows anything."

"Are you going too?" Zoe asked.

"I don't know yet. No. Maybe. I don't know."

"Won't it be dangerous?"

"Look, we don't know anything. Hopefully, it won't be. We talked about her being careful, maybe going at night. But it'll be a risk."

She nodded sagely. "I understand."

They filled the rest of the day watching TV and reading. Marcus only watched with one eye, his mind trying to figure out whether he should stay or if he should go with Ingenue. One thing he decided was that Ingenue should go to the pub at night: maybe early evening. There would be more chance that the pub was open and Robert was there. And if Ingenue's eyes were still sensitive to light, then she would not be disadvantaged should the weather be fine.

Ingenue emerged at dinner-time and showed them the progress so far. She'd almost finished—the tasteful floral pattern was a perfect candidate for her summer dress. She'd cut it into a square top with a flaring skirt, and when she finished off the seams, Marcus thought it could almost pass for store-bought. Over the meal of reconstituted beef stew, they discussed the plans, Ingenue agreeing with Marcus's assessment of going at night. When she mentioned that the remaining work on the dress should be completed by midday the next day, they tentatively arranged for the great expedition to begin early the next afternoon.

Marcus had been tortured the whole day, going backwards and forwards in his mind, weighing up whether he should go with Ingenue. If anything happened to her, then he and Zoe would be sitting waiting in the bunker, alone. And he might be able to do something to help. But if he went, then that would mean leaving Zoe in the bunker alone. Which wasn't something he wanted to do either. Marcus finally remembered William's words on the lake while fishing. He took a deep breath and let it out, and then realised there was no way that he could stay behind while Ingenue went out—that he had to go too. That out of the way, he turned his attention to what to do with Zoe. There was no way that he'd leave her behind, so she would just have to come with them. There, that was settled. Now, the last thing Marcus wanted was to be shot at again, so he would have to hide, following Ingenue from the shadow of the trees. Out of sight. With Zoe. He couldn't let his sister out of his sight, in case anything happened to her. He was responsible.

He let Zoe and Ingenue know his thoughts. Ingenue's shoulders relaxed and she sighed. "Thank you," she said gently. Zoe squealed excitedly.

"Zoe! Listen to me, this is important. You have to do what I say, it doesn't matter what it is, but you have to keep quiet and you have to stay close to me all the time. We don't know who is out there and what they want and we might be in danger. Do you understand?"

She nodded gravely, and Marcus almost believed that she would behave herself.

"What are we going to do for money?"

"What do you mean? Why would we need money?"

"Well, this... Robert did you say his name was? If Robert isn't on your Uncle's side, what do we do then? We can't buy a drink if we don't have any money."

Marcus paused to consider this. "That's true. Maybe we could swap a packet of food for a beer?"

Zoe walked over with an iPad.

Marcus and Ingenue looked at each other.

"Better check them to make sure they don't have something like "Property of Eastwell Manor" written on them anywhere. That might be a little bit of a giveaway."

They collected a few of their favourite meal components which didn't need heating, two of the iPads and put them on the table. A couple of bottles of water joined the pile.

"How long are we going for?"

"Let's assume that we're going for two days."

"Then that's about the right amount of food and drink. We'll try and get a refill from a tap somewhere."

"What about the bandages?" asked Zoe. "Won't people ask what has happened to you?"

"Good point, Zoe. It might be the time for the big reveal. Is there a hand mirror anywhere?"

"Just the big mirror in the bathrooms."

They trooped into her room, stepping over the remnants of pillowcases and the duvet and went into the en-suite. They watched her in the mirror as she started to peel the bandages off. There was silence after she took the last one off. Broken eventually by Zoe.

"Does it hurt?" she asked.

She looked like she'd done ten rounds with a professional boxer. Her eyes were puffy and her nose was swollen. More concerning were the deep bruises along her eyebrow ridge, the sides of her nose and under her chin. She smiled and then let out a little moan. "Only when I laugh. Or smile. I think it looks good."

"Good?" asked Marcus. "What are you going to say if anyone asks about it? 'You should see the other guy'?"

"Wounds received in subduing the enemy?"

Marcus thought for a moment. "That makes a lot of sense. Implies heroic behaviour, which might put people in mind to help you."

"I'll keep the pressure bandages around my body. They help me move more easily."

"Wow, ok. So we'll go tomorrow after lunch. That's the plan. Let's sleep on it to see if there's anything we've missed."

They filled the rest of the evening with yet another movie, this one a throwaway comedy from the previous decade, the plot as far away from anything involving fake identities, revolutions or bunkers as they could find.

The next morning Marcus got Ingenue to sew straps to the spare pair of pillowcases that she hadn't already used, turning them into backpacks. He and Zoe packed the backpacks with the food, water and iPads, while Ingenue worked on finishing her dress.

Eventually, Ingenue came out to model the dress, which turned out to be rather fashionable.

Lunch might be their last hot meal, so they made sure to make it a good one. They chatted about this and that—about some of the costumes that Ingenue had made and helped make at the theatre company. Marcus got some insights into the political animal that was community theatre, but it was obvious that they were just distracting themselves from the upcoming mission. Eventually, they could avoid it no longer and began their preparations. Marcus took care of the dishes and then finished loading up the backpacks with a couple of rolls of toilet paper and some soap.

They formed a dysfunctional group, heading towards the closet with the hatch in it. Zoe led the way, her backpack almost the same size as she was, the phone in her hand scanning left and right. Then came Ingenue, delicately trying to avoid anything which might brush dust or dirt onto her dress or, more dangerously, might snag or tear it. As she said, it might not quite stand up to being washed. Marcus followed, the other backpack slung awkwardly over his shoulder.

Once they started moving in earnest down the corridor, Marcus discovered how they weren't really prepared for the journey. Ingenue didn't have any shoes and would periodically kick or stand on a rock, muttering an obscenity under her breath. Zoe's feet were too small and Marcus's were too big meaning that they couldn't even share their shoes with her, so he just had to wince in sympathy at every collision or bump and hope that the damage wasn't too bad by the time they reached the other bunker.

The air was fresher the closer they got to the end of the cavern and Marcus surmised that whatever opening to the sky was through some small gap in the ceiling high above. They stopped at the ladder and Marcus asked Ingenue about her feet.

"I'll survive," she said through gritted teeth.

Zoe went up the ladder and pushed on the underside of the hatch. It sprang open easily and she disappeared into the small bunker, Ingenue climbing up after her. Marcus watched her feet as she ascended the ladder. She had a few nicks and cuts but, to Marcus's relief, they were superficial. When she was at the top of the ladder she turned and Marcus handed up the two food backpacks.

They all stood awkwardly in the bunker for a second before Zoe broke the ice.

"Do you need to use the toilet?"

Ingenue smiled at her and made use of the facilities, washing her hands with the soap that they had brought along.

When she was ready, Marcus led the way to the door. "Now or never, team. We'll be in the woods behind you, Ingenue. Stay off the main roads if you can."

EXECUTING THE PLAN

Ingenue led the way from the bunker door in the middle of the meadow to the gate opposite the cottage, Zoe and Marcus following about thirty feet back. That was too far away for them to see what she could see, but close enough to follow the reactions from her body language. As she reached the gate, they saw her head turn quickly, as if detecting danger, before raising a hand haltingly in greeting. She started to glance back at them, before thinking better of it and climbing the gate. Once over the gate she wasted no time and headed along the lane towards the fish farm. Marcus mentally kicked himself. They hadn't discussed directions except to indicate that they should head west, and here was Ingenue wandering off by herself. They also hadn't worked out any way of communication with hand signals which was another oversight. Had she seen someone? Why was she walking that way?

Marcus grabbed Zoe's hand and hastened to the gate, ignoring the memories of the bullet zinging through the air the last time. They arrived just in time to see Ingenue disappearing up the lane. Marcus helped Zoe over the gate and then crouch-walked over to the hedge which separated the lane that led to the Cottage from the field with the fish farm. He could just make out a figure descending the catwalk leading down from the top of the fish farm containers. Was it Graham?

He found a spot in the hedge which was particularly thin and pushed his way through, scratching his arms in the process. He turned and held some of the branches so that Zoe could get through. It was easier for her, being smaller. In the distance, he could see Ingenue crossing the cattlestop and entering the pasture. Marcus's heart was in his mouth and he truly expected a shout accompanied by a gunshot to erupt at any time. William's voice echoed in his ear though. Marcus was committed and he had to make the plan work. He wanted this. He could see that the figure from the catwalk was in fact Graham and that he was talking to Ingenue. He didn't seem to be armed. There was no chance of overhearing what they were saying from this distance.

Ingenue looked around. She waved back the way she had come, and called out, her words lost in the slight breeze. Marcus assumed that meant that it was safe to come out, but he didn't want to risk Zoe's life if he was wrong. He crouched down beside her.

"Hey Zoe, I'm going to go over and talk to Graham and Ingenue. You stay here. If anything happens to me and Ingenue, I want you to make sure it's safe and then go back to the bunker, OK? If everything is OK, I'll do that silly dance from that cartoon you like, OK?"

She looked indignant. "It's not a cartoon, it's the Plane People."

Marcus summoned a smile. "OK, but you know the dance right?"

Zoe nodded.

Marcus dashed across the open ground between the hedgerow and the shipping containers, taking advantage of the fact that Ingenue and Graham seemed to be focussing their attention on the cattlestop in the opposite direction. Marcus stealthily made his way past the shipping containers to the closest point to where Graham and Ingenue were standing and then crouched down, listening.

"I'm not sure where he is, he's supposed to be following me."

"And you're sure it's Marcus? The Rebel guy shot at him and I was worried that he'd been hit."

Marcus stepped out from behind the containers. "No, he missed," he said.

"Jesus!" exclaimed Graham. Ingenue jumped as well.

"It's good to see you, man. I was really worried. I went over to where we saw you that day that the guy shot at you, but couldn't see anything, so I hope he'd missed and you'd got away."

"By anything, you mean a body or any blood, right?"

Graham coloured a little, but didn't say anything.

Ingenue interrupted. "So what are you doing here anyway?"

"If the fish don't get fed, then they die. So I'm making sure they stay alive. That's my job."

Marcus looked at him warily. "So you don't have a gun? Nobody's going to shoot us?"

Graham spread his hands. "It was the other guy, not me."

Marcus nodded. "OK, I believe you. One minute." He walked a few steps away from Ingenue and Graham and performed the Plane People dance, which involved circling an imaginary airport with his arms outstretched like wings. He only did a brief version of the dance and then rejoined Graham and Ingenue, ignoring their disbelieving looks. A few seconds later Zoe joined them, coming around the side of the shipping containers along the same route that Marcus had taken.

"Tell us everything," said Marcus.

Graham looked from Marcus to Ingenue to Zoe before proceeding. "Look, there was nothing we could do—they had guns."

"From the start," Marcus interrupted.

"OK, so I'd be hearing rumours that something was going to happen, but didn't think anything of it. When the protests turned violent, people started thinking that things could really kick off. I was rostered on for the Saturday after the Friday night when the burnings and shooting started, so I just turned up for work as per normal. There was a guy I hadn't seen before who told me he'd be 'looking after me'. He had a rifle and stood up on the catwalk most of the time, looking through his telescopic sights. I saw him freeze and start taking aim so I yelled up at him just before he started shooting. That was lunchtime on Saturday."

Ingenue looked at Marcus who nodded. "Yeah, that was me."

"Yeah, he was really pissed. He went over to see if he could see a body, but he was pretty sure he missed. Apparently, he wasn't to leave the fish farm area, so he didn't go any further and came back straight away. I got in so much trouble for that, I thought he was going to shoot me. Eventually, he calmed down, but not before telling me he was going to report me as being a sympathiser. That weekend, no newspapers were delivered, none of the supermarkets took deliveries and the shops ran out of the usual stuff. Toilet paper, flour and eggs. That guard guy slept in his car and was here when I came back on Sunday. And again on Monday. I don't know what he was eating, but there was a cooler in the back of his car alongside the sleeping bag, so I guess he was well-prepared. By Tuesday we heard that the army was patrolling the countryside, hunting down the death squads. I didn't know that there were death squads, but I guess the arson across the countryside couldn't have all been set by single guys with rifles, right?"

"The whole weekend was weird. There was a delivery of newspapers with Insurrectionist propaganda, and then nothing. The phones hadn't worked since the uprising, and the internet was really slow. We could get some news though, so we knew what was going on. The army started liberating towns one by one and there were reports of firefights and battles, but it was pretty much one-way traffic. The rebels were pretty much defeated by this point and I think they saw the writing on the wall because by Monday I turned up as per normal and there was nobody here. Marie turned up to work and told me about the mansion." He turned to Marcus. "I'm so sorry—there was no sign of your Uncle or Aunt."

"They were taken away," said Ingenue.

"Oh, so maybe they're still alive," said Graham nonchalantly. Realising how flippant that had sounded, he continued. "Oh, I mean, I'm sure they're fine. The guy who was stationed here was talking about re-education camps, so I'm sure they're teaching them about the new world."

"Do you know where the camps are?" asked Marcus.

"I'm afraid not. One last thing—we heard a whole bunch of gunfire on Sunday. Yesterday everything pretty much went back to normal—supermarkets started getting replenished and all the newspapers were back. Still no cellphone coverage though. That's supposed to come back this week sometime."

"What day is it?" asked Zoe.

"It's Tuesday the 27th of July," answered Graham soberly.

Marcus and Ingenue came up with the answer to the unasked question at the same time.

"So we were in the bunker for twelve days," Marcus said.

"Bunker?" asked Graham.

"Never mind. Do you have the internet on your phone?" asked Marcus.

Graham shook his head. "No, it uses the cellphone network, so it won't be back up until mid-week. There's an internet cafe in town. Actually, it's just a computer in the closet of the local greengrocer, but he lets you use it for an hour for a couple of quid if you promise not to download porn on it. It's on the edge of town, just past the Duck's Bark."

"Oh, can you show us where it is?"

"I can't leave the fish, I have to monitor the oxygen levels and finish the feeding, but I can give you directions if you like?"

"How have you been getting here? I can't see your car."

"I usually got dropped off and then a rumour was going around that it was unsafe to be on the streets. We never did find out whether it was the army or the rebels who were shooting up cars, but Marie and I agreed to leave the car at home and I walk here each day. She obviously hasn't had to come into work since... well, you know."

"So is it safe on the roads then?" asked Marcus.

"I hope so. I've been walking here and back each day. You should be fine."

Ingenue looked doubtfully at Marcus. They got directions from Graham and waved goodbye before heading back towards the burnt-out cottage, chatting as they went and trying to establish the safest way to travel.

"I think we'll be ok, as long as we stay off the main roads. Maybe we just walk through the fields and keep the road in sight all the time. That way if there are any death squads patrolling we'll be alright. And by the sounds of it, they should all have been arrested or killed in firefights with the army."

"Are you still saying I should go first? And you follow in the bushes with Zoe?"

"Well, I guess if we're off the main roads then we can all travel together. It should be fine, right?"

"I hope so," answered Ingenue.

They passed the burnt-out cottage and took the lane to where it met the main road. From here, if they turned left then the road would meet up with Lake Road and from there they would turn right and walk a few miles towards town. The Duck's Bark was on the outskirts of town, before the idyllic rural countryside turned into suburbia. They agreed that they would cross the road where it joined the lane and go maybe a hundred metres or so into the fields to move parallel to the road. If they had to climb fences or go through hedges to stay off the main road, then so be it. They still had plenty of time to get there before dark and the weather was behaving. The day was mild with tufts of white clouds sprinkled across the sky. No danger of rain.

They dashed across the road. On the other side was a wood of thin silver-barked trees. There was a fence but it was very overgrown and only a single strand of wire was visible above the weeds and brambles. They made slow progress through the wood. The trees were sufficiently spaced, but the tangled summer undergrowth made making headway hard work. Further away from the road there were fewer brambles, allowing them to make better time.

"Is this far enough, do you think?" asked Marcus.

"Any further and I think there's a good chance that we might get lost," answered Ingenue, wincing at the beating that her feet had taken getting through the recent terrain. While Marcus had tried to protect her fragile dress from the forces of nature he'd only been partially successful, and one of the seams was starting to loosen. The carpet of grass and flowers where they were now was much more soothing than the dried brambles and ferns.

They continued on without complaint or incident for about an hour before the woodland gave way to open fields. Far to their left, they could see the road, an immaculately flat topped hedge marking its edge. About the same distance again on their right, the wood edged the field, putting them in the middle of the short side of a long rectangle with a farmhouse directly opposite them.

"Around or straight through?" asked Marcus.

Ingenue shrugged.

"I can't be arsed going around, so let's go straight. It looks easy going."

They headed towards the middle of the field. As they got near, they could make out a shape lying on the ground closer to the townhouse ahead of them. It was the size of a body and directly in their line of travel. Marcus realised that they were very much exposed out here in the middle of the field. They hadn't heard any cars at all along the road, but if someone had happened along they would definitely be seen. They crouched down for another conference.

Marcus didn't want to bring up the shape ahead in case it did turn out to be a body.

"Shall we get into the treeline and skirt around the farmhouse?" he asked Ingenue.

"Why have we stopped?" asked Zoe.

"We don't know whether we should go up to the farmhouse or skirt around it, Zoe," he answered.

'We could ask that man who is dressed like a tree over there. I think he's been following us," replied Zoe.

Marcus and Ingenue slowly rotated until they faced the same way Zoe was facing—towards the long side of the rectangular field. She was waving in the direction of the woods. Marcus followed the direction of the wave and sure enough, one of the trees was waving back. The man in the ghillie suit was holding a rifle in the other hand. Marcus felt his legs turn to water and it was everything he could do to stay upright.

"What do we do?" hissed Ingenue.

"I don't know, he's coming over!"

The man was indeed coming over towards them, placing the gun on the ground on the other side of the fence before climbing over and collecting it. The scene reminded Marcus of a lava lamp, the man once part of the forest now a tree out of place in the otherwise featureless field. Or, more accurately, a green Wookie striding across the paddock.

As he got closer they could see that he was about forty, slimly built and both blinking and sweating profusely. He wasn't wearing any camouflage makeup which struck Marcus as peculiar. All the characters in computer games that Marcus had played had faces smeared in matching dark or green face paint to complete the picture.

"What's the password?" asked the man gruffly.

Marcus stared at him in horror. The man had a gun, was blinking uncontrollably and was demanding a password.

"Nobody told us. They just said to meet them at the Duck's Bark, so that's where we're going," Marcus found himself responding, his voice much steadier than he thought it would be.

"Nah, the rallying point is at the farmhouse here. Who told you to go to the Duck's Bark?"

"Dunno his name, he was at the fish farm."

"That'd be Trevor, he's a muppet. Look, you can't go into town, too many people have been turned. They're all turning against us. They were all supposed to join in, once they saw what we could do. A once-in-a-lifetime opportunity and they just can't see it. A chance to make a change for their kids and their children's kids. All wasted. And now.... It's the last chance. The last stand. Do you have a gun, boy?"

Marcus shook his head. "Trevor said something about getting one at the Duck's Bark. We should really be heading over there."

The man frowned. "This is supposed to be the rallying point. If anything happens, we're to meet here. I've been patrolling and keeping it safe for us," he nodded toward the body closer to the farmhouse.

"I don't know what to tell you, Trevor said to meet him at the Duck's Bark and the fact that he isn't here means maybe the plan changed and nobody managed to tell you."

"I heard gunshots. A lot of gunshots, a few days ago. I was hoping that wasn't Trevor and his team," he pulled down the zipper at his chest and wriggled the hood of the suit back off his head. He was balding and his face was a deep maroon with rivulets of sweat running down his cheeks. "I guess that might mean you're right. I should probably come with you, right?" He paused to wipe the sweat from his head with his sleeve, the tendrils of camouflage leaving little tufts of olive and khaki cotton embedded amongst his thinning hair.

Ingenue looked alarmed, but Marcus was ready for the question. "You've already got your gun—besides, what would happen if others turn up here because Trevor's message didn't get to them? Best you stay. We'll let them know that you're here."

The man hadn't told them his name, but he didn't seem to realise that. He also seemed to be a little affected, but Marcus still didn't know whether that was from the heat or a pre-existing condition. All he could think about was how to talk his way out of this encounter, how to get to the Duck's

Bark without him, and how to leave the field so that Zoe didn't see the body lying on the ground closer to the farmhouse. He was by now convinced that the body was a result of the ghillie-wearing sniper standing in front of him.

The man thought for a while before nodding and wishing them good luck. He started walking towards the woods where he'd come from and Marcus led the way for Zoe and Ingenue, cutting a forty-five-degree angle away from the farmhouse and leading them into the corner of the rectangular field that lay furthest from the road.

As they walked, Marcus half-turned and told Zoe to keep an eye on the man, a little concerned about what he might do but more of as an excuse to prevent her from looking at the body to their left. Once they reached the corner of the field, they halted and Marcus asked Zoe about the man.

"Oh, I saw him for a while. Sometimes he'd look through his eyeglass, but whenever he did that I would wave at him and he'd put it down again."

Ingenue looked around concernedly. "Aren't you worried about him? What was all that about passwords and such?"

Marcus nodded. "Yeah, I was a little worried, but if I acted like we were on his side, then I figured we might be able to bluff our way through."

"Weren't you worried about telling him where we were going though?"

Marcus coloured a little. "I panicked and said the first thing that popped into my head... I'm not a good liar."

"OK, well, should we get going? We don't want to be around when he changes his mind and decides that we aren't his friends, right?"

"Yeah, true. Zoe, is he following us?"

Zoe looked around and frowned. "No, but... What is that?" she asked, pointing into the sky.

They looked up as one. High above them, something was circling the field. It was the size of a large bird but its wings did not flap. It was some sort of drone.

"Time to go," said Marcus and helped the other two over the fence which encircled the field. On the other side of the fence, the woodland continued briefly before again opening out into another field. They carefully made their way through the trees before repeating the fence-crossing ceremony and breaking into a quick jog across the other field. Behind them, they heard yelling, which echoed over the countryside making it impossible to determine how many people were yelling or what they were yelling about. They broke into a sprint, making haste across to the gate on the other side. The gate took them to another road—Lake Road if Marcus's navigation was correct. They crossed the road and headed into the field on the other side before swinging right and walking parallel to the road which remained visible through the hedges. A screen of trees rose high above the road and undergrowth. The trees meant that they could tell where the road was even from a distance.

By this time they were no longer sprinting but loping along in a fast walk. They'd just finished walking through their first pasture on this side of Lake Road and were halfway across the fence when gunshots rang out in the distance. They froze. Silence immediately resumed. The silence of a world watching and listening to see if any further violence would be forthcoming.

The rest of the way to the Duck's Bark proved uneventful enough, though they kept an eye out for any strangers. Occasionally they would see a farmhouse and would navigate the best they could around it, not wanting to bump into anyone. It wasn't until they reached the familiar carpark outside the Duck's Bark that Marcus started to think about what the plan should be for entering the pub. Who should enter and what should their story be? Normally at this time in the day early diners should be starting to arrive for their meals. But who knew how much custom Robert would be getting under the current circumstances?

Marcus briefly contemplated Ingenue going in alone, or the two of them leaving Zoe hidden in the bushes outside, before deciding that they would all go inside, surely they'd be safer together. They'd bluff their way through and depend on quick thinking to figure out what they would do.

Taking a deep breath, Marcus pulled the door to the pub open and stepped inside.

REUNION

It took Marcus's eyes a few seconds to acclimatise to the shaded interior of the pub and, by the time they had, Zoe had already sprinted past him and was hugging Aunt Meredith. She had been sitting in one of the booths and had clambered out upon seeing Marcus enter. She now stood with Zoe clinging to her. Marcus was not slow in joining Zoe, giving her a hug on the other side. On seeing Ingenue standing awkwardly nearby, Marcus gestured for her to join them, creating a ball of noisy hugging.

Zoe was babbling, trying to tell Aunt Meredith everything that had happened to them. Aunt Meredith was crying, kissing each of them in turn, with a brief look at Ingenue in confusion, while Marcus was just happy that the nightmare was over. But where was Uncle Reggie?

In one of the pauses, while Zoe drew breath, he asked the question out loud. "Aunt Meredith, where is Uncle Reggie?"

Aunt Meredith's happy tears turned sad. "We still don't know. Sit down, all of you, have some food, you must be hungry? Robert, three more for dinner," she called out.

"Are we safe here?" asked Marcus, aware that if the man in the camouflage suit had escaped the firefight that they had heard then he may very well be on the way to the pub.

Robert had come out to see what the ruckus was and gave Marcus's hair a tussle. "Don't you worry about that, my boy, we can look after ourselves here at the Bark. Three burger meals coming up!" And he disappeared into the kitchen area. It gave Marcus an opportunity to see the inside of the pub.

Things had changed a little since his drunken night, which felt like a lifetime ago.

The various farming implements that once adorned the walls ornamentally had been taken down and put in front of windows for protection. Some of the tables were on their sides near the doors, as barricades. The effect was to make the restaurant look like a western saloon with the baddies outside and the goodies holed up, waiting for the final assault. There were no other customers or waiting staff around either.

Aunt Meredith took a deep breath and composed herself. "OK. I'll tell you everything that has happened in the last two weeks, but some of it is a little upsetting, Zoe, so I need you to put your brave girl face on, OK? So, Uncle Reggie came back to the house and said that there were some people coming who meant us harm. Typical Reggie understatement. He sent William and Francine away to their family's place, and they took off. You know he sent Ingenue away as well. Then the bad men arrived. They were going to shoot us before one of them turned out to be one of the boys on the fish farm and he spoke up. He said that we weren't old money and that we should be taken to the re-education centres. After some discussion, while Reg and I damn near peed ourselves, there was agreement. So they split us up and took me to a golf clubroom. I have no idea where they took Reggie. There were only women there. It started off with maybe a half dozen but after a few days that was up to about twenty. There wasn't much to eat and the crowd was starting to get a little restless. I think by that time the uprising was taking a bad turn, as the number of guards was halved. Then an army unit turned up and captured the guards. They took everyone's statements and then said we could go."

She took another deep breath. "I walked back to the Manor. But there was nothing there. A burnt-out husk. No food, nothing. So I left a note on the gate saying that I would be here and got a room upstairs. I bought a laptop at a shop in town and have been trying to find you guys and Reggie on all the online notice boards and chatrooms ever since. What happened with you all?"

They all spoke at the same time which was impossible to follow, so Zoe told her side of the story first which was somewhat of a roller-coaster but in no way made it clear what had happened. Marcus waited until she had finished and then stepped in.

"After we saw what happened at the Earl's, Uncle Reggie sent us to the bunker."

"What bunker?" asked Aunt Meredith.

"The bunker in the meadow in front of your cottage," responded Marcus slowly, frowning in confusion.

"There's no bunker in the meadow in front of..." Meredith trailed off in thought. "Ah, my birthday present. We'd been out of the country in the States, negotiating a movie deal in the week before you guys came over. Reg kept on hinting at some sort of present for my birthday that was being organised while we were away. He got me a bunker?"

"Well, I don't know anything about when he got it or how, but it wasn't really set up to be used, so it makes sense that it was newly installed. Anyway, he sent us there to wait and hide. He said it was well-stocked but there was no food there. I was a little upset."

Zoe started to speak, but he stopped her with a glare.

"And so I went and got Ingenue from the mansion. And then took her back to the bunker. And by then Zoe had found a hatch to a second bunker."

Aunt Meredith frowned. "Reg got me two bunkers?"

Marcus shook his head. "No, the other one was under the mansion. And that one had the food in it."

"I'm confused. If Reg said that there was food in the bunker and there wasn't, but that there was food in the other bunker which was actually under our house, how did the food get into the second bunker?"

"I think I know. If the same company installed both bunkers, then they would know about the bunker under the mansion, right? And then if they asked Reggie where to put the food he had just bought, he would have just said 'in the bunker', right? And if one bunker had this big room especially for food, they would have thought that it made sense to put it in there, expecting Reggie to know about the second bunker." Ingenue looked from Marcus to Meredith uncertainly.

"It's a bit of a stretch," responded Meredith doubtfully. "But I guess it's the only explanation. I'm so glad it was there and that it kept you all safe. And I guess you came out and found the sign, right?"

"No, actually, we didn't. We figured that nobody knew what Ingenue looked like under her bandages, so it would be safe to come out and see what the situation was."

"You're our recovering patient!" Meredith snapped her fingers as she realised how Ingenue fitted in. "I'm so very glad you're alright! I was worried sick about you. And you two too of course my dears!" she added as Zoe and Marcus looked at her.

"So we bumped into Graham at the fish farm, and by the sounds of things the emergency was over and it should be safe enough on the country roads for us to make it here to see if Robert knew what was going on. I remembered from the time we had dinner here that he seemed to like you and Uncle Reggie, so I thought he might be on our side and might be able to help us find you both."

"Yes, the rebels have been pretty much put down across the country by now," Meredith continued, nodding.

"Except we found one," continued Marcus. Meredith's head whipped around so she could look at him.

"What do you mean?"

"We were walking through fields, just in case it wasn't safe, and we came across a man in a camouflage suit. I managed to talk our way out of it, but he was a little intense. He was waiting there for other rebels. I think the army caught up with him because we heard gunshots after we left him."

Meredith's eyes widened. "You were very lucky," she said. "It's been long enough that almost all the rebels have either been killed, arrested or melted back into the population, so the countryside should be back to normal by now. Stories like yours are very uncommon now."

Ingenue was confused. "Lucky because we saw him, or lucky because we got away?"

"Both," said Meredith.

"And so, what now?" asked Marcus.

"Well, we'll get you on the phone with your mother to let her know that you're alright. The phone networks should come back on later on this week, but until then the landlines will work. The internet is so slow that video calls aren't working too well—lots of delay and echoes and you might as well be on the phone. Then we'll get you a room here at the Bark, and I guess we'll wait here until Uncle Reggie comes back. I think there's room here, we can check with Robert."

Zoe piped up. "You can stay with us if you like, Aunty Meredith. Our bunker is big enough. It's quite far, but we've got a kitchen and lots of cartoons. There's plenty of room."

Meredith smiled at Zoe and gave her another big hug. "That sounds nice. Maybe we'll do exactly that. It'd be cheaper, right? And we can be closer to the farms, to make sure the bees and the fish and the chicken are all alright. Oh! We should be able to get you two replacement passports, and if you want to leave straight away we should be able to change the date on your return flights when they start running again next week. If it gets too stressful for you staying here after all you've been through."

"And what about you, Aunty. How are you holding up?"

"I'm just worried about your Uncle, that's all. If I could swap the mansion and the estate in exchange for having him with me right this second, I would."

Marcus patted her arm. "We'll find Uncle Reggie, don't you worry."

"So you're both safe now," said Aunty Meredith as Robert set down a lemonade for Zoe and a pint of the Special in front of Marcus.

"Almost," Marcus agreed, eyeing the pint suspiciously.

EPILOGUE

Two years later, Marcus was in Sydney, seeing the sights and reflecting on his adventures in England. When Zoe and he had arrived back in Auckland at the end of their holiday they had enjoyed a certain celebrity as 'the kids who had survived the uprising' and other hackneyed headlines. The celebrity status had faded within a month and life pretty much returned to normal. High school gave way to University and it was now the short gap between the end of lectures and the beginning of the exams, and Marcus really should have been studying. But he wouldn't have missed Sydney for the world. Zoe's school exams meant that she couldn't make it, which had resulted in a few tantrums.

He was reminded of the bunker when he had arrived at Sydney Airport. He was reminded of it on his first morning when he took the ferry across to Manly to check out the beach. He was reminded of it again that afternoon when he took the bus out to Bondi for a walk to Coogee, and again on his return to the hotel where he was staying in the centre of the city. The city was constantly reminding him of the bunker because it was plastered with posters of Ingenue's movie, "The Bunker", and tonight was the Australian premiere.

Marcus stood in the bathroom of his hotel room, staring in the mirror and struggling with the bow tie. The studio had paid for the flights, hotel and the tux rental, but not one of Ingenue's retinue were around to help him with the cursed thing. He'd spent the morning checking out the Opera House and the historical centre of the city before taking a ferry across the harbour and walking back across the Harbour Bridge. Ingenue had been in back-to-back interviews, a pair of meeting rooms in the hotel having been converted into studios. One room was being set up with the television cameras and lights as she spoke in the other, and as soon as the assigned time was up she headed into the second room, each interview slot just enough time for the crew to pack down and the new one to set up.

Marcus made sure that he was at the assigned meeting place in the hotel foyer at the correct time, even if the bowtie was loosely attached and sitting at 45 degrees. All was calm there—just a few guests checking in, the water glinting over the water. And then chaos.

First of all the male co-star of the movie came sweeping through the foyer, surrounded by a swarm of attendants. They barely paused before heading outside where a big black SUV collected them and headed out into the traffic. And then it was quiet again. A few of the attendants who weren't going to the premiere returned inside, one or two of them tersely chatting on Bluetooth headsets, looking every part like very well-dressed schizophrenics.

The hubbub at the lifts warned him of her arrival, the Bluetooth crew drawn to her like minor moons to a gas giant. She swept into view, trailed by three or four young women dressed casually which only served to accentuate Ingenue's elegance and glamour.

She wore a red dress, with a matador jacket over the top. The dress featured a bustier which accentuated what didn't need accentuating. Its hem came to just above the knee. She had her blonde hair pinned up, with tendrils cascading down, perfectly framing her face. She saw him and beamed. Her smile faltered momentarily and she turned slightly to share a word with one of her attendants.

"You look stunning, Ingenue," he said.

She curtseyed. "You don't look too bad yourself, Marcus." The attendant she'd spoken to inserted herself between them without interrupting their conversation and wordlessly and effortlessly tied his bowtie. "Shall we?" she asked once the tie was in place. She took his arm and they headed towards the door, attracting curious stares. Her SUV pulled up and they boarded, a minder sitting in the front with the driver.

Once they were settled and buckled in, she turned to him.

"It is sooo good to see you! It's been a crazy month, the only thing keeping me going was the thought of seeing you here."

"Mental! You've been in hotels and red carpets for the past month?"

"Answering the same questions, trying to give them some sort of unique spin. The studio has been good, they got me a coach right at the start and they gave me some media training. Chaos the whole time, but the circus means that something is going right with the movie."

"Ah cool: so maybe a sequel?"

She blinked in surprise, before realising that he wasn't in the loop when it came to her career. Grinning, she shook her head. "Maybe in three years. I'm booked up that far in advance. I'm going to get maybe two weeks between press junkets for one movie and pre-production on the next one. My agent says to strike while the iron is hot, and Ingenue is red hot."

It was his turn to blink in surprise. "You're talking about yourself in the third person now?" he grinned. "You've changed, man!"

She grinned back. "Speaking of changing, you've certainly filled out since the bunker. You must be fighting the girls off."

"Nobody special at the moment," he said.

"Well, wait until the newspapers come out tomorrow."

"Two minutes," the minder in the front called out.

"What do you mean?" he asked.

"You'll see. Success brings scrutiny. Scrutiny brings interest. Interest brings opportunity."

Frowning he tried to follow her logic. He was about to press her when the minder was hopping out and opening Ingenue's door. Marcus opened his own door and waited. The swarm of photographers behind the temporary barrier started taking photos, their flashes an almost constant stream of explosions. Marcus was just thinking they were at fever pitch when the minder brought Ingenue out from behind the SUV and placed her hand on Marcus's arm. He was blinded by the constant flashes and so let Ingenue lead them both forward. The photographers yelled questions and Ingenue steered Marcus towards the crowd.

The closer they came to the penned-in photographers, the less the flashes burned into his retinas and soon Marcus could see again. Ahead of him, the big-muscled and coiffured co-star was talking to a camera crew, while his date stood respectfully out of camera shot.

Another TV crew was closer, and Marcus could see that Ingenue was leading them in their direction. As they got closer, a young blonde woman in blazer and skirt held out a microphone and called out. Ingenue smiled and continued towards them, holding Marcus's arm.

"We've just spoken to Lance Reardon, who plays your co-star Articus in the movie. So hot! What was it like to be rescued by such a hunk?"

"Actually, we're lucky enough to have the guy who Articus was based on, right here," Ingenue answered, indicating Marcus with her free hand.

"Oh! Was there as much romance in reality as there is in the movie?" the reporter asked, holding out the microphone to Marcus.

He blinked in surprise. "I think that they might have taken a little artistic license with that part of the story," he managed.

The reporter looked disappointed. "Articus, you're here with Ingenue tonight, are you a couple?"

Marcus looked over to Ingenue and smiled. "No, but Ingenue is a very dear friend, and it's always great to see her."

She smiled back, touched by his words. "I'm not dating anyone at the moment, I'm focussing on my career. But I am very excited to share the movie with the inspiration for Articus. Obviously, it's taken a long time to get the movie made, but I hope we've done it justice. It was very important for us to..." Marcus zoned out as the interview continued, Ingenue handling the questions with aplomb. He looked around at the scene, the photographers and interviewers roped off from the red carpet, and the celebrities slowly making their way along it, pausing for an interview or close-ups. Hangers-on and attendants, of which he realised he was one, stayed trapped in the orbit of their respective stars, and he idly wondered what it would be like if you mapped out the path that each of the attendees would take in relation to their principal. A gentle pressure on his arm indicated that Ingenue was ready to continue and he let himself be led by her further along the carpet.

"Were you scoping out the local eye candy?" she asked with a wicked smile once they were out of earshot of any reporters.

"Just giving you space to do your thing," he replied. They paused a number of times more before reaching the entrance to the cinema. Marcus stood to one side with the other plus-ones and waited while the stars and the crew had an ensemble photo, Ingenue standing out in her red dress against the black and white of the tuxedos. As she returned to him and they climbed the stairs to enter the cinema proper, he asked her why she'd chosen a dress the same colour as the carpet. Surely she was worried about blending in?

She started, worried that he was right and she'd somehow chosen wrongly, before realising that he was winding her up and laughed, punching him lightly in the arm. They went inside and watched the movie, Marcus enjoying the story and nudging Ingenue whenever the inaccuracies were particularly egregious. At the end he had to admit that, for all its faults, it was a rollicking adventure and Ingenue was very good in it. They headed back out into the Sydney evening to find that the red carpet had been rolled away and the hordes of photographers had been dispersed. Only a few camera crews lurked, interviewing anyone they could to round out their stories. One such trio managed to intercept them prior to returning to their SUV. The reporter, knowing that she only had time for one question, elected to ask it to Marcus.

"What was it like rescuing Ingenue?"

"Oh, I don't think I rescued her," replied Marcus. "If anything we rescued each other."

ABOUT THE AUTHOR

C.G. Lambert was born the second of seven children and raised in South Auckland, New Zealand. His pre-writing career consisted of applying for whatever job sounded interesting, leading to time as an International Banker, a Music Manager, Web Developer and Analytics Manager. He loves travel (you can read about it at etrip.tips), holds dual citizenship (NZ/UK), a Bachelor of Arts and an MBA. He currently resides in the UNESCO City of Literature—Edinburgh—with his long term partner.

You can find out more at cglambert.com

WHAT HAPPENED TO UNCLE REGGIE?

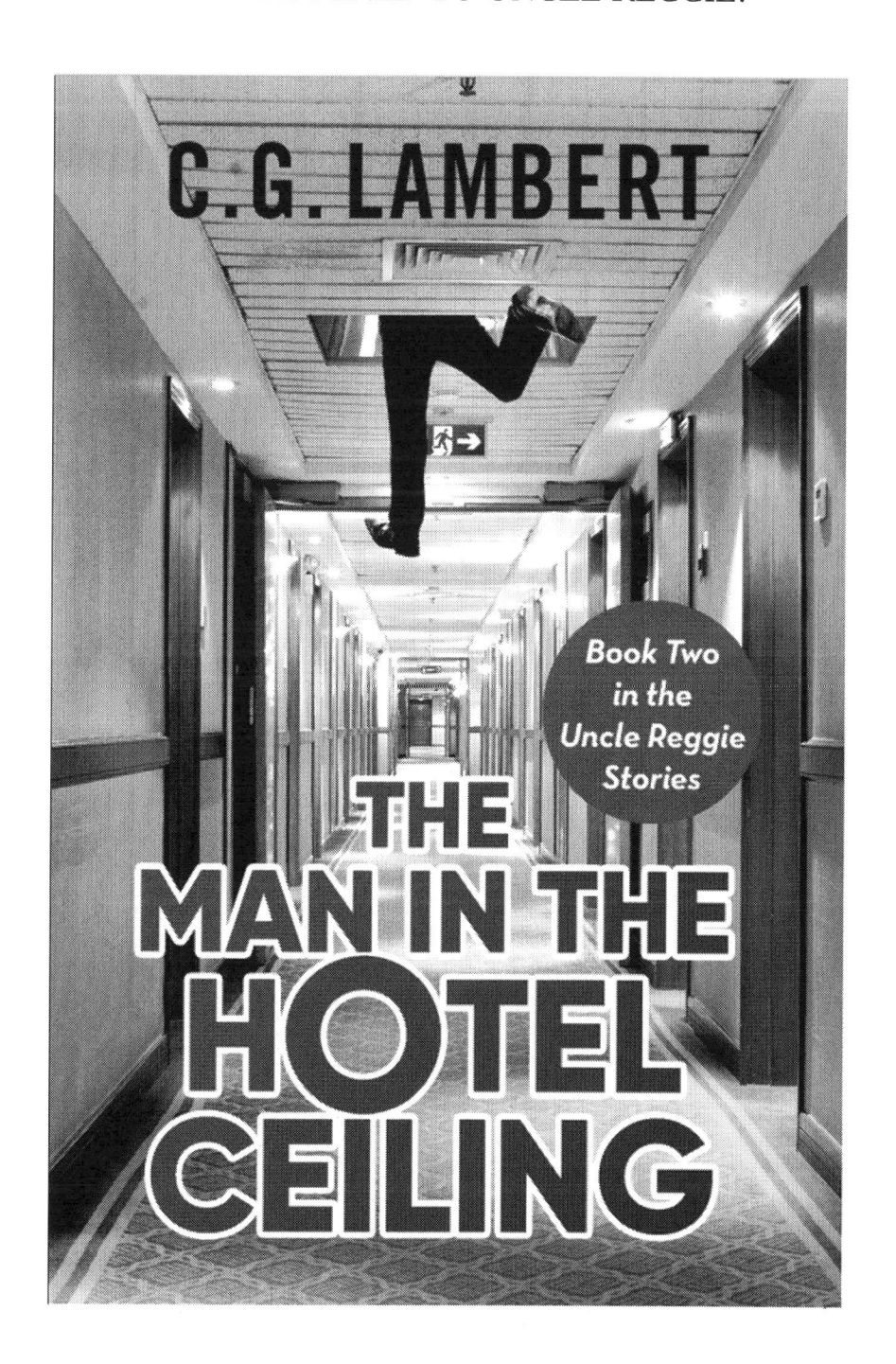

C.G. LAMBERT

Book Two in the Uncle Reggie Stories

THE MAN IN THE HOTEL CEILING

THE THRILLING CONCLUSION

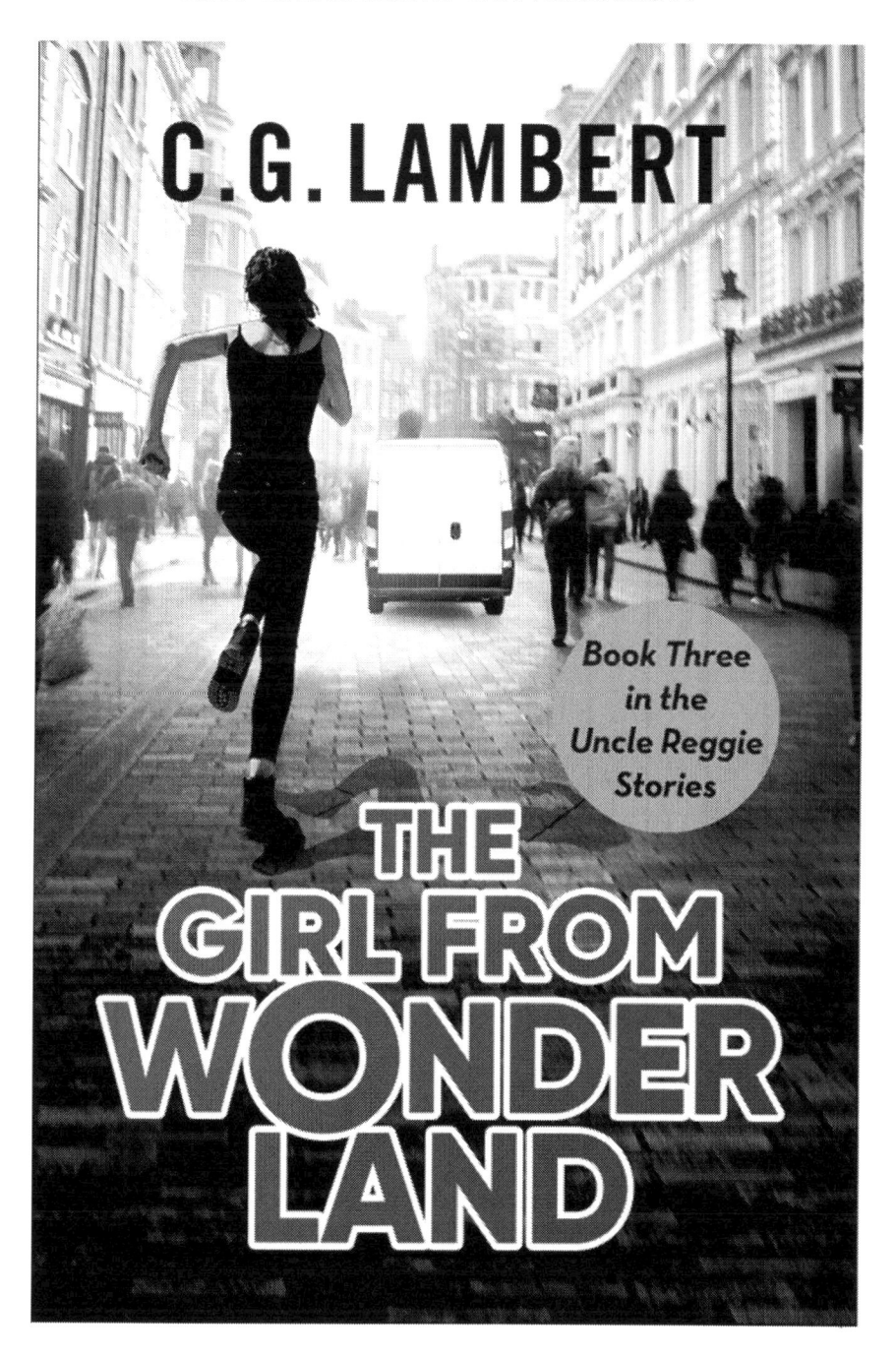

C.G. LAMBERT

Book Three in the Uncle Reggie Stories

THE GIRL FROM WONDERLAND

Printed in Great Britain
by Amazon